PAPIER MÂCHÉ JESUS

KEVIN L. DONIHE

ERASERHEAD PRESS
PORTLAND, OREGON

PAPIER MÂCHÉ JESUS

ERASERHEAD PRESS
205 NE BRYANT STREET
PORTLAND, OR 97211

WWW.ERASERHEADPRESS.COM

ISBN: 1-62105-075-0

ACKNOWLEDGMENTS:

"All Children Go to Hell" appeared first in *Amazing Stories of the Flying Spaghetti Monster* anthology, "Happiness is a Warm Gun" in *The Magazine of Bizarro Fiction #4*, "A Loathsome Job" in *Dragons with Cancer* (on-line) and *Budget Press #5* (print), "Scholar's Note from a Book Now Lost" and "The Vibrant Tools of Dr. Imago" in the *From the Bowels of Birch Street* chapbook, "Death-in-Life Love Song" in *Psychos: Serial Killers, Depraved Madmen, and the Criminally Insane*, "Compassion" in *Nightmares*, "Veronica in the TV" in *Dark Discoveries #8*, "Paul and the Computer" in *Electric Velocipede #4*, "Swimming in Endless Night" in *Chimeraworld #1*, "The Boy Memorial" in *Champagne Shivers #5*, "Seven Part Sunday" in *The Journal of Experimental Fiction #37*, "Master Remastered" on Bizarrocentral.com, "Necrowave Oven" in the *Falling From the Sky* anthology, "The Fast Food Diaries" in *Asylum III: the Quiet Ward* anthology and "The Will of the Dresser; the Will of the Blender" in *Sick: An Anthology of Illness*.

AUTHOR'S NOTE:

This is a short story collection. (I enjoy stating the obvious.)
One story is from my teenage years. Eleven are from my 20s.
Seven are from my 30s. Zero are from my 40s. As of this
writing, I'm not there yet.

-- Kevin L. Donihe

TABLE OF CONTENTS

ALL CHILDREN GO TO HELL

Bored and lonely, Robbie moped in his pale blue room. He'd broken a vase out of spite, and his parents had banished him, indefinitely, to his train-shaped bed. There was to be no TV, no snacks. He was permitted to read, but books didn't interest him. Hours later, he still sat on his mattress, fists propped against his chin, staring at his chest of drawers and thinking about the world outside.

Suddenly, his window flew open. Through it glided a monster of densely coiled pasta, chunky tomato sauce atop its head. Lips formed a doughy smile as the monster regarded Robbie with oversized meatball eyes. Standing before him, it seemed larger than the room.

The boy was confused, but didn't feel threatened. The monster looked funny and smelled of Spaghetti Os, his favorite food since kindergarten. Nothing so silly and delicious would hurt him, he figured.

After nearly a minute of silence, Robbie asked, "What are you?"

A sonorous voice replied, "I am a spaghetti monster."

He then asked what it wanted.

"To show my best friend a magic trick." It paused, cocked its head. "Are you my best friend, Robbie?"

Words failed the boy, so the spaghetti monster said, "I know everything. Become my best friend, and I'll prove it."

But Robbie already had a best friend. His name was Ben, and together they played ball, caught and killed bugs, and built forts of pillows and snow. It seemed wrong to abandon Ben for a creature he'd just met—but he wanted, more than anything, to see magic on an otherwise gray and boring day.

"Yes," Robbie said, finally. "You're my best friend."

"So rub me. See what I can do."

Robbie sat there, staring. What it had said reminded him of the things sweaty, balding men told little boys in weird videos his parents had made him watch. Again, he thought of Spaghetti Os, but still trembled as he left the mattress and reached for the monster.

Beneath his fingers, individual pasta strands felt electric and throbbed like veins. When he rubbed, the strands became motile, twisting around and spiraling into one another as the monster grew. Soon, it was bigger than the house—the Earth—yet expansion continued. Faced with noodles longer than river systems, the boy stopped rubbing.

"Now enter me," the monster said. "It's warm and cozy inside."

Robbie thought food should enter people, but then recalled gingerbread houses where storybook characters lived. Perhaps this was a similar arrangement, and who else in his school could say they'd been inside a spaghetti monster?

"Will I see guts?" he asked, sheepishly.

It laughed as belly strands parted like a curtain. Climbing inside, Robbie found a cavernous hall of white. It was indeed warm and cozy, no guts to be seen. Ahead of him, runners of spaghetti stretched out, knitting together to form a crude hammock. Robbie first sat in it, but his eyelids grew heavy, and he decided to rest.

His mind began to wander, so much so that Robbie forgot he had another home. On occasions, he saw himself outside the monster, but nothing beyond it seemed real. Dinnertime with parents was a gray blur with gray people with fading faces. Whenever they spoke, they said nothing of interest. School was more of the same. Other times, a different, younger voice would call to him, ask him to come out and play, but Robbie couldn't give it a name.

"You are ready," the monster said. "Now close your eyes."

Robbie did, and images snaked out from behind his lids, forming scenes. He saw himself bow before a litany of golden idols, men on trees, crosses, and a massive black cube. He saw himself burn incense and lie prostrate on prayer mats, then confess his sins to dark men in dark rooms and count beads in a rosary, over and over until his fingers bled. Then he clutched a knife—long, curved and glistening. Lifting it high, he let sunlight play on the blade before plunging it into the guts of a tied-down, struggling bull. A moment later, he slid a different knife across the throat of a GI Joe.

A thousand such scenes converged in his mind, meshing into a shaft of blinding white light. Bathed in it, Robbie could no longer think, no longer feel. He'd become all things at once.

No time and forever passed. Dimming, the light separated into component parts, returning the boy to consciousness as idols, prayer cloths, knives and beads were absorbed into the monster to become pasta again.

Suddenly, a booming voice: "You must leave me now."

"But I just got here," Robbie said, disappointed. "Can I stay longer?"

"No one can remain inside me forever, but don't be glum. I have another trick to show you."

Robbie perked at the promise. The first had been better than anything on TV, so he could only imagine how much greater a second trick might be.

Strands parted for him. He saw light, got up and stepped toward it, into a world where his room had become a soggy, decaying ruin. Windows had shattered. The ceiling sagged as brown-green mold grew wild on the carpet. Paper had dried, turned black and peeled from the wall. It littered the floor like dirty snow.

Robbie considered calling down for his parents, but knew they weren't there. Though the place was nothing if not vacant, it didn't concern him; his best friend had a new trick to show.

"Do it! Do it!" Robbie said, impatiently, and was surprised by the depth of his voice.

"I will, if you'll do one last thing for me." The strands of the monster's lips formed another, wider smile. "Make me your *only* friend."

Robbie opened his mouth, but closed it quickly. Perhaps it was best to have friends not made of pasta, sauce and bulbous mounds of meat, friends who didn't want him all to themselves. He thought hard, recalled a forgotten name, and felt a sudden twinge of regret.

"But Ben—"

"Ben has been gone for a while now," the monster said. "He's in a better place."

"He is?"

"You could go out and make new friends, of course—but why bother? I'm already here, aren't I?"

Robbie nodded.

"So do as I ask, and I'll show you the trick."

The offer was too tempting to refuse. "You're my only friend," Robbie said, and meant it.

The monster beaconed. "Then step up; rub me again."

Robbie obeyed, and the walls of his house collapsed and turned to dust. Rotting beneath him, floorboards buckled before giving way. But he didn't fall into the basement. His one and only friend supported him even as it performed the same trick in reverse, becoming smaller than Robbie, then smaller than an infant. In seconds, the monster fit neatly in the boy's cupped palm.

Strands no longer pulsed; sheer electricity felt like mere static. Robbie rubbed with a single finger now, rubbed until the monster resembled an ant. Then he stopped, fearful that he might crush such a tiny and seemingly delicate thing.

"Don't worry, Robbie," it soothed in a still, small voice. "Nothing can harm or take from me. My essence is eternal."

Robbie didn't know all the words, but understood the gist, so he continued until it seemed that he held only air. The trick, he realized, had actually been a disappearing act.

"That was great!" he said. "Now show me another!"

From the emptiness in his palm, there came no reply.

"Are you there?" he continued.

Silence deepened, swallowing background noise. He glanced around, but saw that direction itself had failed him. There was no longer up or down, left or right. He had only his body and a void as eternal as the monster had once seemed. Immediately, he felt lost and alone, trapped and deceived. Dread took hold, then panic and all-consuming horror. Aimlessly, he flailed.

But in time-that-was-no-time, even terror died. Left with his thoughts, he studied the dark hairs and dry cracks of his withered hands. He wondered if his monster had been wrong, if he'd crushed it, if it was dead, or if it had even existed at all. Vision fading, he yearned for all the things he'd left behind, just for the promise of a little magic on a dull, boring day.

"Mom? Dad? Ben?" he called, voice breaking, but they were nothing.

And, in an instant, Robbie was nothing, too.

HAPPINESS IS A WARM GUN

Today will be a better day.

Those words were in Bob's head as he awoke, even as veins in the ceiling throbbed and a dirty old grandfather clock swung a massive penis, once a pendulum, and leered lasciviously with twelve numbered eyes.

He tried not to think too much about this, or the alarm that attempted to seize his fingers with a crab's pinchers as he stretched, or the lamp that resembled a shaded sea cucumber and extended diaphanous filaments to snatch a fly. He couldn't change these things, but he could adapt to them. For too long, he'd carried himself like a thief in his own house, huddled up in closets or the bathtub, not eating, often naked, crying and screaming. It was time to prove that he was stronger than his possessions and live as best he could.

The first thing to do, Bob figured, was get dressed, as would a normal person on a normal morning. He arose, carpet fibers brushing willfully against his feet, tickling them.

The wardrobe was a swollen mushroom, but the dresser had been itself for two consecutive days, a minor miracle. He opened a drawer, reached down for his clothes, and a t-shirt reared up, flaring green and mossy sleeves. It wrapped around Bob's hand. He grabbed it, pulled. The thing wound tighter, but Bob tugged until there was enough in his hands to start ripping. On the floor, cotton fragments shook until they stilled.

I killed my shirt, he thought and wanted to chortle, but bit back the impulse. He'd given into it too often lately.

Instead, he regarded his other garments. Drawers brimmed with active clothing that would never stay on his body. Belts and ties slithered; dress shirts flapped and belched; pants bubbled and oozed. All that remained unaltered were a pair of khaki shorts and navy blue briefs so old they might have been from his high school days. Bob winced as he pulled them over his hips.

Dressed, he walked into the hall past light fixtures like shrunken heads and into the living room where he tried to ignore the toadish armchair and the shrieking fireplace's yellow teeth. He was on his way to the kitchen, as the second thing one did on a normal morning was either eat or defecate. Shitting was out of the question; his bowels were empty.

It was crucial that the refrigerator be uncorrupted, not like yesterday when he was too cowed to use it. *Please, please, please*, he thought, an internal mantra. *Please, please, please.* But fists clenched; he stomped his feet. The fridge appeared as a huge, slumping block of cheese, riddled with holes that emitted plumes of steam.

Still, he reached for it, dreading the act, but imagining the food inside might still be edible. The handle was spongy. It pulsed in Bob's grip as he pulled.

Inside, a jug of orange juice sat on a rack once metal but now flesh. The jug scowled, its lid-mouth moving irregularly, angrily, sloshing oily black orange juice. A glassy pink worm, an ex-butter dish, swished a wilted broccoli tail. A bottle of dressing had swelled alongside an ancient meatloaf. The resulting fusion resembled a translucent puffer fish, studded in ground beef.

Bob closed the door. If he couldn't eat, then he could

brush his teeth. He ran his tongue across them, felt grit and plaque.

On the way to the bathroom, he thought the words again, meant them, even as a drawer from the end table sprouted bat wings and flapped about the room:

Today will be a better day.

The toilet had transformed into a huge, rippling larynx. Bob took some perverse pleasure in urinating into it as it gurgled. Afterwards, he stood in front of the mirror and studied himself, his body so scrawny and disgusting, like something that might blow away with the wind or come up from the earth.

Looking down, he saw that the toothpaste tube was flat, and what little paste remained had hardened. He reached for the toothbrush. Its handle was red, wet and corded, like an exposed muscle. Bristles were dirty brown, swaying slightly and thick as straw. They smelled like sulfur. No matter. He brought them to his mouth and scrubbed. Pain blossomed; he had to scream. The brush, he threw into the sink.

Bob looked at his shredded gums and at his red, clown-like smile. It wasn't the face of someone making a change in his life. It wasn't even the face of a sane man. He just walked away from the mirror, did not wipe the blood from his lips. There was no use.

Perhaps ending the day early was the only way to improve it.

Back in the bedroom, the penis clock still counted away the hours, but the lamp had become itself again. This didn't matter to Bob. He thought only of the rifle in the closet.

He threw open the door. A young, tow-headed woman sat where the firearm had, knees against her chest. She looked at him but did not speak.

"Are you...the rifle?" he asked.

The woman nodded, though he couldn't tell if her answer had been yes or no. When she stood, Bob realized she was naked. Embarrassed, he looked past her, into the closet. The rifle wasn't there.

As soon as the woman left the bedroom, the main doorway in the hall became a jagged and enraged mouth, chomping incessantly. She continued toward the living room. Bob called out, covered his eyes, but the entryway stopped gnashing just before she passed beneath it. He followed her warily, expecting the mouth to return and crush him.

The living room seemed upset that Bob's brains were not on the wall. Even wingless objects took flight, and the fireplace had dislodged itself to stumble around like a squat stone dwarf. Unfazed, the woman entered the room, and, one by one, flapping things lost their wings and fell to the floor. The fireplace's teeth retracted; it shot back into the wall. Shrunken heads became light bulbs.

Now, they sat at the kitchen table, Bob on one end, the woman on the other. Her hands rested on the table, long white fingers laced together. Her face—pale, oval—was expressionless. He just looked at her, trying to aim his stare at her eyes. They stared back at him, not offering a threat, just a puzzle. In front of her, everything was clean. Behind her, the refrigerator remained a lumpy monstrosity, leaning farther to the right, melting over and onto the stove, spreading its plague.

"I'm really hungry, so,—uh,—you don't suppose you could..."

She stood and granted his yet unspoken wish.

Bob hurried to the refrigerator. The interior was chilly, and food inside looked fresh, unmolested. He shoved slices of cheese, handfuls of cold cuts and meatloaf into his mouth. It didn't matter if things that should be warm weren't. He drank almost a full liter of cola, consumed three cups of chocolate pudding. It was nice to have something inside his stomach. For the first time in weeks, he felt solid, *tangible*.

He was so wrapped up in eating he almost forgot about the woman. Turning, he saw her watch him. "Sorry," he said, and wiped his mouth.

Satiated, Bob felt almost clearheaded, and, after shaving and fixing his hair as best he could, devised a plan for the morning. He only hoped it would work.

The woman stood by a window, looking out, he imagined, at all the terrible things he couldn't bear to witness. He watched her for a few minutes, guiltily admiring the curves of her back, twiddling his fingers and biting his lip. Finally, he spoke.

"I wondered if... I mean, if you don't mind... I think I'd like to go out for a drive. Just a short one."

She turned from the window. This time he led, guiding her back to the bedroom where he put on shoes and a shirt and rummaged through newly restored clothing so she might have something to wear. Nothing was suitable, most of the garments too manly and wide, but he chose a pink button-up shirt, a pair of shorts matching his own and a belt to hold them.

She shook her head at the selection.

"I know they're mine, but, if you go out, you're going to need some clothes."

She shook more adamantly.

He returned the clothes to the dresser. "Okay, I guess I can try to explain if we're pulled over."

At the front door, Bob paused. It had been days since he'd tried to leave, and the last time hadn't been pleasant. He steeled himself, opened the door and peeked outside. Something black and shadowy whooshed down, nearly decapitating him. He drew himself back quickly. Through the window, he watched elastic tree branches smack at the porch, whipping from side to side like angry men.

The woman grasped the knob. Bob fell back, and the tree ceased its thrashing as soon as she stepped outside.

He followed close behind her, looking out at a world that would have left him babbling had he been alone. The roofs of the neighboring houses were topped with weathered statues and gray gargoyles rather than antennae or chimneys. The houses themselves were brown and slouching. Below, grass was a fiery red. Above, clouds were grinning, gaseous things. Bob watched a bird fly into one and never emerge from it.

The woman started down the porch. As she reached the last step, grass within a few feet of her became green. Clouds directly overhead: fluffy and white again.

In the driveway, the car was no longer a car, but a shaggy almost-dog with black matted fur, red headlights for eyes and a hideously extended exhaust pipe for a tail. Its bloated tires were claw-studded.

Bob pushed a button on the key ring, heard the sound of the door unlocking, and was amazed it still functioned. "I—I think you should get in the car first," he said, turning to the woman.

The moment before she touched the handle, a rudimentary arm, the beast became a late model Toyota, pale blue with rust spots.

* * * *

Bob traveled through a world of change. It was only just outside the windshield where normality prevailed. Beyond, the road was a whipping serpent lined with natural and man-made atrocities, some entering the roadway as if to challenge the Toyota, only to return and transfigure when it approached them.

He glanced into the rearview mirror and watched the bad things reestablish themselves, filling in behind him like a wave moving at the speed of the car.

The woman just looked out the window, hands in her lap, something akin to a smile on her face.

"Thank you," he said. "I just wanted to say that."

The smile widened.

The Toyota entered the downtown area. While there might have been people amongst the rampaging buildings, automobiles, light posts and newspaper stands, it was hard to be sure. Every transformed thing was monstrous. Just ahead, a car was a sleek, black coffin on wheels. The driver, if it could be called as such, was a windswept skeleton, gray hair blowing on a bone scalp.

Bob drove around a park bounded by a circular intersection, curing the people and things around it, at least temporarily.

"I just want to sit here for a few minutes," he said, pulling into a space by the park, "watch normal people do normal stuff."

And so he stared at people exiting and entering buildings, reading newspapers on benches, waiting for buses, and at construction men repairing pavement, police directing traffic past the work zone. The world remained ugly a few feet to the left of the park he'd circled, but all those who entered the bubble became as themselves again, and things that shouldn't move were unable to cross.

"They don't know how good they have it," Bob said, shaking his head. He almost wanted to leave the car, wander about, but it felt too early still. Even before the changes, the thought of interacting with a mass of humanity had troubled him. He reached for the ignition. "Okay, I've seen what I wanted to see. Let's go back."

The woman placed her hand over the keys.

"What?" he said.

She pointed.

"The park, you mean?"

Her voice was soft yet emphatic. "Yes, the park."

He was taken aback. "You talk?"

Turning from him, she opened the door.

"But you're naked!"

She stepped out. Beyond the window, a finger beaconed.

Bob sighed, left the car. He walked with his head down, but a passing mother didn't cover her child's eyes. A policeman on the other side of the road looked his way but kept going.

They reached the entrance. Beyond, the park was small though pleasant, ringed in trees. The woman guided him to a bench by a pond where a paddling of ducks swam. A weeping willow drooped its branches over its left corner; a wooden railing bordered its right. In time, Bob was almost able to forget the city.

"This may sound dumb," he said, "but I've always liked ducks. My mom, she'd take me to the river when I was a kid, and we'd feed them."

There was a tap on his shoulder. He turned, saw the woman's outstretched hand, a slice of bread in her palm.

He didn't question this, just took the offering, tore it into pieces and threw it to the appreciative ducks. "I'm glad you made me come here," he said. "It's good to go out. It's just... I'm not a very confident person. Things are safer when I'm alone." He looked at her. "But maybe that's not true anymore."

He heard something behind him, turned quickly. An elderly couple had entered the park. They appeared content as they walked hand in hand along a circular cobblestone path.

Bob scratched at his neck, debating whether or not he should speak his desire. "Can I hold yours?" he asked, finally.

"You may," she said.

His hand trembled but he linked it with hers, watched the ducks and contemplated all the things he'd lost but might regain, turning possibilities over and over in his mind until the sunset colored pond water red and gold.

Night had fallen before Bob returned home. Though dark, he could see that his box was stuffed with mail, mostly bills. He claimed them before unlocking the door.

Inside, things were in the process of changing again—upholstery looked slick and oily, wallpaper flapped and the TV had grown legs. Bob allowed the woman to enter first.

"Hey," he said. "Fix the TV and maybe we can watch something."

The woman passed it and continued into the hall.

"Wait. Come back."

Just prior to entering the bedroom, she turned. Again, her finger beaconed.

Bob didn't know what to make of this. He dropped the bills, followed her. Pausing at the door, he saw the woman on the bed, back against the headboard, one leg crooked at the knee. His stomach felt heavy; sweat broke out under his shirt.

"No TV," she said. "Undress."

"But I... I—"

She repeated the demand.

He obeyed, but didn't remove his briefs.

"Now come."

Legs quivered as he made his way to the bed. It was ten feet away, but seemed more distant. "Are you sure?" he asked.

She tapped a finger on the mattress.

He sat down on it, covered himself up with sheets quickly, embarrassed that the woman was seeing so much of his body.

She pulled the sheets back down. "Don't," she said.

"But look at me."

"You're fine," she said.

"No, I'm not."

She stroked his cheek. He pulled away. She leaned over, kissed him on the mouth. He closed it tight. Then a hand was in his underwear. It gripped his cock, squeezing, moving up and down. Forces he thought he'd never feel again started to build inside.

"Surrender," she said.

It had been so long since he'd been with a woman, but he couldn't allow himself the pleasure. It was too good for him.

The hand moved faster, tenting blue cotton. "You will surrender."

"But I... I'm a bad man."

"You're not."

He tilted his head back. "God," he said. "You're so beautiful." Then he let his mouth gape.

Slowly, she maneuvered herself atop him.

From the living room, Bob heard the crack of wood and the shriek of metal. It sounded as though the two were grinding against one another, compacting. Never had the things in the house been so angry. His penis began to wilt in her grasp.

"Don't listen," she said.

There was noise like clomping feet. Bob turned to the door. Through it, he saw a composite monster. It bounded into the hall, a juggernaut that moved on coat rack legs and flung carpet-roll arms muscled with furniture. The stove was its belly, the fireplace its head.

"Don't look."

"But—"

She pressed her hips into his. "Love me," she said. "Love yourself."

Bob swallowed fear, penetrated her while the monster raised an armchair fist over the bed. The fist slammed into Bob; he felt only pleasure. The monster roared as its component parts loosened, fell to the floor and shattered.

At that very moment, the woman pulled Bob's trigger. He shattered, too. Like bullets, his fragments plowed through and obliterated the things he thought he knew. Time passed without his knowledge until, naked and sweaty, he coalesced in a brighter world. A somehow familiar place, where women were women and guns were guns.

A LOATHSOME JOB

I loathe work. My boss, M. Makulahbaum, is supposedly a dentist; I'm supposedly his assistant. I don't know a damn thing about dentistry. I don't believe he does, either. He's never filled a single cavity or capped a crown or shoved things into sleeping and/or euthanized patients. In fact, all he does is float around in the form of a red mist.

A sign above his door says:

M. MAKULAHBAUM, DENTIST
Where nightmares of flesh and bone collide
* * * *

I enter the foyer to his office and take the steps up. A song plays on the intercom. Makulahbaum blasts it each time an employee walks through the door.

I reach the final step. The chorus gets so loud it penetrates me. My body ripples with data and pulses to a synchronized beat. I slam my head against the wall, harder and harder, until my brain rock n' rolls right out of my skull and into a deposit box by the door.

Makulahbaum refuses to let employees carry their brains to work. It used to bother me, but I've gotten over it. Mine is usually riddled with little holes when I get off, like something long and hard has been rammed into it, perhaps for hours, but I don't need a brain when bathed in the light

24

of Makulahbaum's office. It infuses me, reaches into my synapses, finds the soul inside the machine and has its rough and tumble way with it.

Inside the reception area, I utter the customary greeting one uses when entering a workspace:
"Baby, I'm back! Use me!"
The secretary and a passing custodian drop what they're doing and clamor toward me. They run claw-like fingers over my body and use words like 'ripe' and 'succulent.' I brush past them, entering the office where Makulahbaum waits.

He's a man of Spartan taste. There isn't much here apart from his desk, though he has a rather impressive wall-mounted face collection. I've yet to see one quite like it, and don't think such a thing can be bought retail.

Miniature manatees swim in a tank by the desk.

I take my seat as Makulahbaum floats from his. His soul-body enters mine, producing a sudden electric tingle and the bite of copper on my tongue. He says nothing, but that's to be expected. He's not the talkative sort.

Behind his desk are two identical white doors. I'll enter one or the other; the morning routine never varies. Makulahbaum lets me know, in his special, silent way, that I am to enter the door on the left. Not that it matters. All doors open into the same room.

His mist-body pulls away and floats back to the desk. I get up and head toward the door like a gas chamber gurney or an electric chair sits behind it. In truth, the door leads to an office almost identical to Makulahbaum's, only smaller and without the neat wall-faces and mini-manatees. It's a drab, boring place—painted all in white—and sunrays streaming through the window look gray even when it's night.

The clock says twenty minutes have passed. *They* rarely stay hidden so long.

Not seconds later, something flaps against the window.

Great. They were waiting for me to think about them...

I turn, not wanting to see the wing that made the sound, but knowing I must. It's their usual way of announcing arrival—the penguins that waddle out on the ledge and, on bad days, hover above it.

There are only two of them, regarding me from behind the window, eyes looking past my flesh and into my soul. They hiss at what lies within. I always thought hissing was a trait reserved for cats, geese and certain reptiles.

The first penguin's eyes turn red.

"Stop it!" I bang my fist against the window facing. "I will not accept this!"

The second penguin's eyes do the same; an ethereal flipper curls around my skull.

"Get out of my mind, you ball-gnashers! Leave me be!"

They refuse; three more waddle into view. The ethereal flipper curls tighter. I grab my skull, screaming as my brain swells and breathes. I dash my head a few times against the filing cabinet before realizing there's no filing cabinet, but notions of 'real' and 'unreal' don't concern me, not when those birds fix me with their fucking graveyard-all-night stare-a-thon gaze.

I'm powerless. I can't shoo them off, not when they see past my mask, not when they know who I really am. (*Hell, I don't even know that!*) Any attempt would be feeble, impotent, and the penguins would surely laugh.

I imagine the sound of penguins laughing and my ears bleed a little. In desperation, I launch myself at the window, smacking my body against it so hard the pane rattles. Then I repeat the process, twice.

More penguins. The world becomes a black cave. Everything's dead here. No light. And, god help me, I think I'm dead, too. I'd hoped to make it longer, but I'm going out now, baking under the wilting stare of urban penguins.

It's time to enter my Happy Place and observe events from there. Goodbye.

My watch beeps. The world sucks me back in, and I'm not dead. It's just lunchtime.

The penguins waddle away from the window. They know the drill.

Zip lock bags filled with brown, throbbing blobs lay on a table in the employee's lounge. A piece of scrawled-on tape on the front of each bag reads *work food*. There's no drink, but the food is moist and soppy so I don't need water.

I take a bag and walk up a stairwell to the roof. The penguins are there, sliding down the backs of weathered statues, roosting in the mouths of gargoyles.

I don't remember the roof having statues and gargoyles. No matter. I sit down by the door and hope the penguins understand I'm on break.

They don't bother me on the roof, but are waiting for me upon my return, dozens of them, crammed against the lower half of the window, red eyes aflame, fixing me with their stare.

I face the opposite wall and don't think about them, but feel a presence nevertheless, like a huge and terrible monster is standing behind me. I spin around. One of the penguins levitates at least a foot above those plastered against the pane.

"We are inside you," it says. *"We are you. Let you become us."*

"I will never become you!" Then I hiss at it. I've never before been so bold, especially not so soon after cowering. It gives me a frisson.

The penguin hisses back, and I return the favor. I refuse to let it have the last word. For hours, we hiss in turn.

A Makulahbaum flunkey enters the room. I call him "Dickey" because he wears a necklace of dried, severed penises. I don't know his real name and never see him—or any flunkey—unless I'm needed.

"Makulahbaum says you're free to go." He faces the penguins. "And you guys did an extra good job today, so you'll get a raise."

"Thanks, bub," one of the penguins says through the pane.

"How about me? Do I get a raise?"

Dickey cocks an eyebrow. "Why ask, #4?"

"I don't know. Maybe because I've been taking it up the ass for five years now?"

"Broach that subject with Makulahbaum."

"He doesn't speak!"

"You heard me. I don't have my mouth stuffed full of cotton, do I?" Dickey opens his mouth. At least eight spit-soaked cotton balls fall out.

Negotiating with flunkeys is useless. I face the penguins. "Damn you all to hell!" I shout.

They ignore me, put on tiny hats and coats, and float off, heading north.

* * * *

I almost forget to pick up my brain at the drop box. When I return to claim it, there's a new sign taped to the door:

COMPANY POLICY REVISION: Effective next Friday, leave your heart as well.

SCHOLAR'S NOTE FROM A BOOK NOW LOST

The private life of Elizabeth Snodgrass III remains shrouded in obscurity. While details are vague at best, the comprehension of available facts is necessary before a reader should attempt to digest a collection of her seminal work.

Elizabeth Snodgrass III—perhaps the most enigmatic figure since Jesus Christ—was born in 1846 to Old Mister Snodgrass, an unemployed tobacco merchant who resided in Westonbury, Connecticut. Old Mister Snodgrass was confused as to why he—a man—should be pregnant. By the time of his daughter's anal birth, however, he had decided it best to simply love the child and downplay the situation's inherent weirdness. Old Mister Snodgrass embraced her with open arms and bequeathed onto her his Christian name: *Elizabeth.*

The young girl matured quickly, her precocious development brought on by the fertilizers her father stored in the basement where she often played. Stunningly pale and dangerously fragile, her appearance provided a source of amazement for the citizens of Westonbury. Most viewed her as the epitome of Victorian lasses worldwide and, quite often, snipped away locks of her supernaturally curly hair for use in various potions and ointments.

Elizabeth's popularity only skyrocketed. Ultimately, she found herself in constant rotation at county fairs. There—

alongside her loving father—the future authoress sang Bette Midler covers and donned sequined rhinestone vests to appease the citizenry. (*How she managed to know the lyrics to songs not penned for another century puzzles scholars to this day.*)

On the eve of her twelfth birthday, Elizabeth's world shattered as Old Man Snodgrass lost his life in a wheat threshing accident. Poor Elizabeth looked on as the machine hungrily divorced limbs—one after the other—from his flailing body.

From that point until the winter of 1869, Elizabeth existed in a whirling, cataclysmic hell. She often carved strange symbols into her flesh and showed older boys her underwear without their prior consent. In top-secret written reports, friends describe her behavior as resembling that of a "devil-child" or "voodoo-vixen." Elizabeth was said to dabble in the blacker arts during this period and was even rumored to conjure Satan in a boot every other Thursday.

On Christmas Eve 1869, however, a dread shade emerged from the ritual campfire, consuming two fellow worshipers during what would have otherwise been an ordinary black mass. This unexpected occurrence heralded her conversion to Christianity at age 23. Soon after her baptism, Elizabeth experienced a spiritual reawakening—the first in over a decade spent wallowing in depression and depravity—and wrote such timeless (and frequently anthologized) pieces as *Untitled* and *Untitled.* Prose from this bright era exhibits a fundamental understanding of both the oneness of reality and the multiplicity of perception.

Bolstered both by faith and a renewed lust for the creative process, Elizabeth soon reintegrated herself into society and—like the child she once was—toured the county fair circuit one last time in the Fall of 1871. There, Elizabeth belted out not only the familiar favorites but expanded her repertoire to include songs by *The Eagles* and *Jefferson Airplane.* (Her journal describes this season as "my most blissful hour.")

Elizabeth's cup continued to run over with joy until her ill-fated 1877 guest appearance at Westonbury's annual Fourth of July picnic. She didn't have time to finish the last verse of *Wind Beneath My Wings* before her legs fell off for no apparent reason. Elizabeth did not take this sudden loss well, and, after cursing both God and Baby Jesus in the same hot-dog scented breath, once again spiraled into the pit of madness.

During the subsequent black years, Elizabeth tended to ignore writing in favor of rendering drawings indicative of a terminally diseased mind. The stories and poems she did pen, however, were imbued with uncharacteristic vitriol and transgression. A number of these pieces—rendered under the pseudonym *M. Mollypants*—somehow managed to worm their way into otherwise staid periodicals (*i.e. Lady Mountback's Home Journal, How Young Ladies Might Impress Their Gentlemen Suitors,* and *Chatterfield Lady's Gazette and Perfum'd Scent Emporium*).

The literati responded by lapsing into psychosis. They could not take Elizabeth's fierce *karate-chop* against the status quo and responded to her threat with only the harshest invectives before committing suicide *en masse.* Old ladies ran their wheelchairs into moving stagecoaches. Men in knickers hung themselves from rafters as fathers drowned their sons in the River Thames. The literary world fell into ruin.

Needless to say, this controversy brought Miss Snodgrass much fame and attention among those she dubbed *the powers that be* and *those who pull the strings.* Elizabeth claimed these shady figures probed her in many hard to reach places and often flew above her house in stealthy, black shuttles and dropped propaganda leaflets onto her yard both day and night.

It is obvious that her alliance with these men of questionable reality transformed her mental collapse into full-blown physical decay. By age 35, Elizabeth was no longer capable of making adult decisions. Spending her remaining years in an upstairs bedroom, she composed ghastly parodies of verse—only to lose these lines beneath the drool-torrents that seeped onto the pages from her prematurely withered mouth. One of the few poems from this era to survive is reproduced below:

Shaving my Lovely Donkey

> i am shaving my lovely donkey.
> do not attempt to stop me.
> nothing shall stand between me
> and the shaving of my lovely donkey.
> oh, how i love to shave my lovely donkey.
> watch how his lovely donkey hair
> falls to the floor and gathers in piles.
> lovely donkey, speak to me.
> say my name.
> who's your daddy?
> i am your daddy.
> i am shaving my lovely donkey.

At the time this poem was composed, Elizabeth's only human contact came in the form of her homosexual lover, the charming—yet domineering—Countess Maria Standish of Lendenthorpe Manor. Sadly, the Countess used poor Elizabeth for little more than perverse, bestial fucking and, in 1886, abandoned her to join the circus.

Now completely alone, the authoress crawled even deeper into her brain, denying any and all forms of social interaction until she was a strangely powered shell—dead, for all intents and purposes, yet somehow going through the most basic motions of life.

During her final year, 1889, Elizabeth boldly edited—some might say, "slashed away at"—her prose in every published copy and original manuscript she possessed. She referred to these alterations as *Hidden Text* and, in her insanity, believed them to be secret messages transmitted to her by an inter-dimensional commune of circus midgets.

Two examples of *Hidden Text* are listed below:

Original Text (from *Voluptuous Sunrise*):

It was about mid-day when I saw him. He was smiling and his hair was turning gray. He didn't see me as I passed. He never does. The man always seems so distracted, like there's something on the ceiling.

Now, with *Hidden Text* in **boldface**:

It was about mid-day when I saw him. He was smiling and his hair was turning gray. He didn't see me as I passed. He never does. The man always seems so distracted, like ***he's got a ferret in his pants.***

Scholars agree this *Hidden Text* was Elizabeth's attempt to distance herself from a past in which she could no longer find solace. The more she tried to run, however, the more quickly she fell into disrepair. By the summer of 1889, Elizabeth's back crawled with green pustules from having spent three straight years in a feces and urine soaked bed. Blood poisoning was imminent. Her imaginary doctor friend (who, as her journal reports, visited her every night) announced on August 25th that she had exactly two weeks until her body shut down completely.

But Elizabeth fought the inevitable and survived for *fifteen* days—gleefully cheering her twenty-four hour old triumph over the non-existent doctor's prediction. When the town coroner pulled her body from the bedroom, she weighed a mere fifteen pounds and had managed to develop what doctors of the day dubbed a *venom gland*. The medical community was hard pressed to explain why Elizabeth hadn't expired eight to ten years earlier. Professionals in the field speculated the incident might be "supernatural in origin." (*Registry of Human Voices*, 1890, **Used with permission**)

After her body was removed and her room cleared out, the following poem—her last ever—was found adhering to the underside of her filthy bed sheet:

> I need to write a word or two to tell you how I feel,
> but since it's all a game of shit,
> I think I'll fold this deal.

A week later, Elizabeth was buried atop a hill in Westonbury—mourned only by a tax collector and an irate she-goat. History records that her body was dumped into a hole, face first without a coffin. Due to her repeated curses against all that was Holy, Elizabeth was denied a Christian burial. Her corpse was, however, permitted an exorcism as it wouldn't stop moving once put in the ground.

Upon her demise, Elizabeth requested that her poetry be burned and the ashes spread across the grave of her sainted father. Rather than comply with these wishes, her more dubious family members locked Elizabeth's work in a private vault, where it remained until 1984. That year, scholars—in conjunction with numerous covert government officials—collected Elizabeth's personal records from her money-grubbing descendants. Hence, the tome you are presently reading was conceived.

This anthology stands as only the second attempt to collect the work of Elizabeth Snodgrass III and the first to incorporate her *Hidden Text*.

– Dr. Charles Cutlery Blummenthal IV
Chair of The Institute for Literary and Paranormal Studies

PAPIER MÂCHÉ JESUS

Six days previously, Truth had descended upon the applicant as he ate with his wife and daughter. One second, he chewed a fatty hunk of meat. The next, he sensed the presence of a divine juggernaut. It surged toward him, crashed up against and meshed with him. It filled his being with light, love and forgiveness everlasting, and it wanted him just as much as he wanted it.

It had a name—*Jesus*.

He knew he had to find and be with this man-who-wasn't-a-man. His wife might go hungry, but she carried enough weight to sustain herself. His daughter had fallen ill prior to this, but her condition would likely improve with the passing of days.

Guilt wanted to tug at him. He rebuked it and departed the village the following morning.

Now, he sat on a stool by a rough-hewn table in a tiny and unfamiliar house where he'd been told the Christ had been secreted.

To his left, a wall-mounted rug began to flap. He jumped as a bald and brawny guard emerged from behind it. His sun-baked body wore a studded codpiece. Leather straps crossed his chest. The guard regarded the applicant with eyes like stone and beaconed him with a forward sweep of his hand.

Then he slipped back into the space behind the rug.

The applicant followed.

He found himself in a short, narrow hall. To his right and left were earthen walls, but another rug hid something at the far end.

The guard's hulking shadow fell over him as he walked. The man smelled, too—ripe and salty. To distance himself, the applicant thought about what that rug concealed, yet experienced something akin to horror as he imagined Jesus asking things of him, judging him and seeing more of him than anyone had ever seen.

Perhaps he should turn back, leave.

But they were already at the end of the hall.

At that moment, the guard pulled away the rug to reveal a sturdy wooden door with an iron handle.

"Is he—there?" the applicant asked.

The guard's voice was sonorous. "Do it."

"Do what?"

"Knock."

The applicant obeyed. A few moments of silence, then the door opened into a deep yet narrow room without windows. Inside, a large wooden chair sat at a long wooden table, accommodating a beyond life-sized puppet, tethered to strings that ran into the ceiling. The puppet was comprised of mounds of thin, bleached parchment, torn to pieces and held together by glue. Features were painted-on.

"Ah," it said, "you received my transmission."

The tinny voice came from somewhere overhead. The applicant looked up and saw something like a black horn mounted on the wall. He lifted his gaze further, but saw no shadows and heard no treading of feet above him. He returned his attention to the puppet.

"I sense you've traveled far to see me," it continued.

The applicant was confounded. Had he expended such energy for this—some trick?

"You're not Jesus," he said, finally.

"But I am, my son. Open your heart and glimpse truth."

"You're not even—"

The puppet smiled, but that was impossible. "Please, sit," it said.

The applicant stood.

"But I insist."

He took an uneasy seat in front of the puppet as it attempted to lace its fingers together. "Most applicants don't have as many teeth as you do," it said. "Congratulations."

"How can you see them?"

"With my eyes. They see all."

The applicant gesticulated wildly. "Your eyes are painted on!"

"Things are as they are, my child."

"Yes, and you're parchment and glue!"

"I assure you that I am of flesh and blood, but I am also three entities, and to serve one you must serve them all." Strings made the puppet's arm gestures seem placating. "It's confusing, I know. Even I find it difficult to keep straight."

"How can you—"

A lifeless yet dismissive hand waved. "Let's cut the chit-chat, okay. I'll lay it on the line for you: I need people. I need feet on the streets."

The applicant tried to process the thing's strange words. Was this divine speech? Did he not have the ears to hear it?

"I've got a good, solid base," it continued. "But, if I can't build on it, then everything's wasted, no?"

The applicant could only nod.

"Ultimately, there are to be twelve disciples. In truth, it doesn't matter how many I choose. I could take you and 12,000 others, but it's probably best to stick with the script."

"Please wait," he said. "I'm very confused."

"Don't fret the particulars. Most of my followers never will." Papier Mâché Jesus reached awkwardly for a stack of papers, attempting to take a sheet from the top. Failing to do so, he swept the entire pile toward him. "There are, however, things you must know.

"The job won't be easy. You'll be gutted and burned alive, hung from trees and thrown to lions. You'll be reviled by the masses. These are givens. To serve me, you must not only be willing to die. You must expect death, then embrace it wholeheartedly."

"I *was* willing, but—"

"Excellent." The puppet paused. "I want you to know something else, though." It leaned in closer; the voice overhead became a whisper. "Things may seem bad— terrible, even—but they won't always be that way."

"What do you mean?"

"I mean, it may suck to be you—but, years from now, your kind will control empires."

"Suck to be me? My kind?"

Papier Mâché Jesus spoke over him. "And, if selected, you'll get your name in a big book. It'll be a bestseller, in hotel rooms all over the United States!" It winked at the applicant.

He recoiled.

"So you see there are perks, too," the puppet continued. "Rest easy in that knowledge."

"How can I do that?"

"By placing complete trust in me. I'm going places. You can, too." An arm lifted. A stiff thumb raised itself slowly. "Keep the faith, my child, and keep on truckin'."

"*Truckin'*?"

It seemed to shrug. "Nothing. You wouldn't get it, anyway."

The applicant wanted to flail. "Please, just tell me who you are and what's happening!"

"I am everything, and everything happens at once."

"Your voice doesn't even come from your body!" He

thought about the wife and daughter he'd left at home, about seeds to be sown and money to be made. He felt anger build; he couldn't contain it. "I think you're a demon, and speaking with you is forbidden!"

"Wrong," Papier Mâché Jesus said. "I'm greater than any mere demon dreamt of being."

"I don't care what you are! I no longer want to be your disciple!"

"My child, please listen closely." The thing smiled widely, parchment cracking around its lips. "What you want is irrelevant."

Dread subsumed rage. "Does that mean I've been... chosen?"

"Only my father can tell you that, but I'd rather not discuss *him*." Papier Mâché Jesus glanced at something strapped to its wrist. "Oh my, look at the time," it said before collapsing as though strings had been cut. Emptily, its head thudded against the tabletop.

The applicant reached out an unsteady hand to shake the puppet's shoulder.

It didn't respond to his touch.

He stared at this thing he'd traveled miles upon miles to see, just in case someone or something would again enliven its strings or that the black horn on the wall would create its voice.

Neither happened.

The best thing to do, he figured, was leave.

The guard was still outside the door, though another man— as bulky as the first—had joined him. He was tall and dark-skinned like an Egyptian, but darker than any the applicant had ever seen. He didn't smell of the toilet or stable, and his clothes appeared foreign, expensive. A shiny black thing worn over his eyes made them look inhuman, like those of a giant insect. Something was stuck in his ear, too. A wire from it trailed down the left side of his face.

The applicant asked the guard, "Where did he come from?"

The guard said nothing.

The insect-eyed man dropped a heavy hand on the applicant's shoulder. "Go well?" he asked.

"I—I don't—I—"

He leaned in. The applicant smelled his breath—fresh, redolent of mint. "If not selected," he said, "you're to tell no one what you've seen and heard here."

The guard's breath was like rotten fish. "Understand him?"

"I, I, I—"

"*Do you?*" he pressed.

"Yes!" the applicant shouted. "Yes, I do!"

Both men pulled back. "Good, and remember," the insect-eyed man added with a smirk, "the Father watches all."

At that moment, *something* seized him and made his head tilt. The ceiling rippled as though dry earth and rushes had become water. Waves formed the face of an angry old man.

Long hair flowed.

Eyes leered.

The mouth opened, and a snake-like thing, fluid and shimmering like oil, emerged. It darted toward and then away from the applicant.

"Go now!" the guard shouted. "Leave here!"

Something released him. The applicant bolted for the door.

He did not look back.

A line of robe and rag-clad men extended from the house for miles.

The applicant couldn't bear to look at the others, couldn't bear to consider the horror they would soon feel.

He kept running.

The village seemed larger than it had upon his entry, as

if its structures had reproduced on ever-unfolding ground. He tried not to think of this. He just continued along the line of men that looked not at him, but straight ahead toward a house now too distant to see.

Cresting a small, treeless hill, he finally stopped.

The queue of applicants ended below, but it wasn't linear. It ringed him in like a box.

His clothes and skin felt tight. He wanted to scream, to take off running and not stop until he'd broken past the line. If someone tried to prevent him, he imagined he would tear through flesh and bone—or paper and glue—without thought or mercy.

But he was too weak in mind, body and spirit to fight. He sank to his knees. Heart pounding, lungs rattling, he feared the line could not be breached, that he'd never again see home or his wife and daughter. His greatest fear, however, was that the Father had approved of him and that he was, now and forever, a disciple of the Lord Jesus Christ.

DEATH-IN-LIFE LOVE SONG

I stand in rain like needles on my skin. I remember you and me, our nakedness, and sex beneath gray and swollen clouds.

We weren't self-conscious. Beady-eyed neighbors couldn't see us over the protective hedge. Even if they did, we wouldn't have cared. Let them live through us. They existed from nine-to-five and would never experience a downpour like we did.

After you left, I hated rain. Darkness coiled around me—oblivion in motion—each time a storm cloud coalesced. There was no pleasure in getting soaked alone.

But now I know his name, and I'm making an unscheduled appearance at 311 Woodcrest as soon as the storm ends and I put on clothes. Must avoid white t-shirts, and that's too bad. I am, you know, a very casual man.

Two hours later, and you're mine.

The apartment was easy to locate. It was just a few miles away. Amazing. You'd been so close for so long.

Unfortunately, the man was stubborn, though it took him a while to notice me. I was quiet, and a glass box had commandeered his attention. He didn't lift his eyes from the screen until I was ready to strike.

My first blow only stunned him. Though his mouth opened and closed like a goldfish, he said nothing before my hammer fell again. A red flap opened on his scalp, but still he staggered, blubbering and drooling on himself like the world's biggest baby.

So I hit him a third time, a fourth, then a fifth. The experience was becoming absurd. Finally, gravity did its belated work and carried him to the floor.

Bent over the man, I noted his upturned, glassy eyes. Perhaps I'd gone too far. Taking hold of his wrist, I detected a pulse. My fingers lingered over it for longer than necessary. Human existence seemed fragile when the highways to the heart were buried in fleshy graves.

I withdrew my fingers. (You know I go off on mental tangents. You said that little facet of me charmed you the most. Standing in the apartment of the man I had just beaten senseless, however, afforded me little time for contemplation.) I struggled a bit to pick him up.

Out of the apartment, I helped him to my car as I would a drunken friend. He *was* well acquainted with the bottle. Though I just met him tonight, I know all about the guy.

You might say I've read up on the subject.

Now, he lies strapped to two card tables pushed together. I never fancied myself a surgeon, but I've done enough research to know cutting through the chest is going to be a bitch.

Wish me luck.

The ribcage is like living marble. Every stroke brings me closer to my destination, so I keep sawing, despite the strain

Hours pass. I want to abandon caution and plow through the body, but I stay my hand. His life force is your life force, and I can't risk losing you again.

The ribcage wobbles. Grasping a segment of it with pliers, I twist back and forth until it breaks. Light illuminates the breach and reflects off of you, Judith, resting inside.

My hands play over you. I feel your death-in-life love song resonate through organic strings. You don't need a mouth to sing. I realize this now.

You lurch beneath my touch. Perhaps I should be gentler. Forgive me.

But also try to understand. After the accident, the mortician used his best tools to construct a smile for you, but putty only goes so far. In your casket, I saw the ghosts of slits and gouges on your sewn-together face.

Smiles, you see, come from the heart, and darkness alone lies in empty cavities. Your seat of love was placed in a cooler and turned into a rush-delivery package. It was shipped off to an undeserving recipient.

And what was left for me? Just the memory of a few hours spent with a shell in a gilded box.

But you're back, Judith. Nothing else matters. Blow the rest to hell.

And guess what...

Tomorrow's forecast calls for rain.

SUPPER WITH VILLAINS IN AN ALTERNATE UNIVERSE

Banks Hatewell (aka Peace Loveman) soaked up atmosphere in a rear booth at Sonny's Bar and Grill.

He relished each visit to Sonny's, even if it meant traveling through the Earthquake Zone to get there. The restaurant was a homey place—richly paneled walls, shiny hardwood flooring, muted track lighting and lithographs of Goya originals hanging above each booth. Banks made it a point to sit beneath the print entitled *Saturn Devouring His Children* whenever possible.

Though the entire restaurant resonated with his taste, he especially liked the oiled, mahogany bar. It was a century old and had been transported to the mainland, via steam-liner, from a haunted Irish pub. At times, when he neared it, he imagined he heard riotous singing.

Little touches like that made all the difference.

Banks looked up at the coo-coo clock to the left of the Goya and realized his dining companions were fifteen minutes late. He hoped Herr Fraknow and Father Malachi would keep their engagement. He hadn't seen them in years and was eager to once again converse with his comrades in crime.

His wait allowed him time to reminisce. What fun they'd had before parting company. Boxes filled his apartment, each brimming with souvenirs taken from various conquests. Banks often rummaged through these, savoring nostalgia's warm glow. His favorite memory, however, was not of their grandest exploit, but of a felonious prank pulled in more youthful years. It had involved a church and ten buckets full of week-old cow guts. Banks sighed. Those were simpler times.

Through the grapevine, he had heard that Father Malachi and Herr Fraknow were no longer on the best of terms. He hoped the rumor was unfounded. It would be a shame if some petty quarrel had driven a wedge between friends.

Banks pulled out a blue, leaf-wrapped cigarette purchased from a homeless man outside the restaurant. He didn't usually take things offered by such people, but he was low on cash and even lower on smokes. The homeless man said something about the cigarette being an "intergalactic recipe" and that he had cranial transmitters attached to his scalp in strategic locations. Banks said nothing and walked off.

He wrapped his lips around the smoke, lit a match and sucked hard. The habit was killing him, but smoking was the perfect way to pass time when there was nothing better to do. He savored the heady, yet somewhat fruity plumes as they clouded his lungs and caused putrescent pre-cancerous nodules to boil atop soft tissue.

Aaaaaaaahhhhhhhh, Banks thought, lacing his arms behind his head. *So satisfying.*

Glancing out over the railing, Banks saw Father Malachi and Herr Fraknow being ushered to the booth. *Finally.*

The hostess escorting his friends was all smiles, but the two men seemed the definition of gloom. Herr Fraknow crunched his hands into fists as Father Malachi cursed under his breath and fidgeted with his Roman Collar. Both walked with a clipped, hurried gait and pretended the other wasn't a waitress' width away.

So much for wanting a pleasant meal.

Fraknow and the Father took their seats and, to avoid eye contact, stared wordlessly at their menus.

Banks felt the urge to say something, but decided to just peruse his own menu. He glanced at some of the more exotic cuisine featured, plates designed for foreign taste buds. His face scrunched. Banks wasn't prejudiced against interplanetary guests; he simply didn't have the stomach for *stuffed zykolp head with agodavo sauce (eyeballs included)*. Instead, he focused on the section that trailed beneath the HUMAN header.

Banks wondered from what section Father Malachi would order. He recalled once seeing a tentacle extend from the man's left ear and slither about his hair. Of course, he had seen this from the corner of his eye, and Malachi had denied everything.

Banks wasn't incredibly hungry so he decided to order the garden salad. He continued scanning the menu, however, because the other two were doing the same.

He unleashed a sigh when the waitress arrived five minutes later.

She beamed. "And what will you have, sir?"

"I'll have the garden salad and a glass of sparkling water," Banks replied.

Snickers enveloped the table.

"What!"

"Oh, nothing." Herr Fraknow did his best Victorian lass imitation. "*I'll have the garden salad. It's the only thing that won't offend my delicate constitution.*"

Banks scowled as the waitress turned her attention from his order to Malachi's.

"And what will you have today, Father?"

"I'll have the T-bone steak—make it bleed. I would also like two bottles of your finest champagne. One for the road."

"And you, sir?"

"That's 'Herr' to you, missy."

"Sorry. And you, *Herr Sir*?"

"I'll have the lobster. But don't dare serve me anything frozen! Take one from the tank and kill it. *Painfully.*"

The waitress nodded.

"And I want an appetizer of Cheesy Potato Skins. I hear your restaurant makes the best in town."

"We sure do!"

He shook his head. "Little people take pride in stupid things." He sighed. "Sad, really."

Though confused, the waitress continued to smile.

Father Malachi motioned her away with an exaggerated sweep of his hand. "You have our orders so you may go." The waitress bowed and scampered back into the almost rabbit-sized hole from which she operated.

"Now that *servant* is gone," Herr Fraknow said, "we can get back to business—which, I do believe, was my wholesale trashing of Father Malachi's reputation."

"We're both men of the cloth! What makes you so high and mighty?"

"Are you saying we're similar? If so, I don't know where you got that information." He took a sip of water, patted his lips dry with a napkin. "I, for one, am not into boys."

"Excuse me?"

"Don't think I haven't heard about that little incident in Tangiers."

"But that was strictly church business!"

Herr Fraknow withdrew a folded envelope from his pocket. "Photographs don't lie."

"*It was business, I tell you!*"

"Maybe your idea of *business* is different than mine. If that's the case, do accept my apologies." He grinned. "But you're still Grade X material."

Though he had already ordered, Banks again lost himself in his menu.

Father Malachi continued to protest. "You have no right to say that!"

"I created and took the financial helm of a worldwide super-religion! You're an everyday, good-for-nothing priest!"

"An everyday, good-for-nothing priest *with practical plans for universal domination!*"

"And I'm sure they look great on paper. Unfortunately, things don't fall into place until you control large amounts of capital."

"Oh really? Nothing fell into place for you, did it? Your statues were torn down in six months!"

"My religion is on a downward slide. So is the economy. Go bitch about that."

"Ooooh. Did I touch a nerve?"

"*No, you didn't!*"

"That's not what your mother told me." Father Malachi nodded to an ancient whore in the adjoining booth, collapsed and stinking of booze.

"Liar! She didn't tell you anything!"

The Father brandished a butter knife. "No one calls me a liar!"

"*Damn it! Would you two kindly shut up?*"

Steely eyes turned toward Banks Hatewell.

"Oh, and who do you think you are? *Peace Loveman?* What a fag-name!"

"Listen here! That was a ruse to fool the tree-huggers! I picked a sensitive lot to blend in with and subvert. Sue me."

"So, did these hippie friends of yours teach you about feminism? Or, should I say, *femininity?*"

"Come on, Fraknow. Open your mind before it suffocates."

"I'd rather not, thank you kindly."

Father Malachi agreed with Herr Fraknow. "Fag. Fag. Fag. Fag," they sang in unison.

Banks Hatewell rolled his eyes. "Guys, let's just accept that we're equals."

"Never!" Herr Fraknow's hands became fists. "Competition keeps the world turning! You're just mad because you're losing the race!"

"Worldly success can't hold a candle to raw ambition."

"Spoken like a true fag."

"Grow up," Banks admonished.

Herr Fraknow stuck his tongue out at Banks. "You first."

"Stooping to that level, I see."

"Maybe, but you're too much of a pussy to reciprocate. You're afraid I'd slice off your tongue if you *dared* stick it out at me!"

Banks sat back. He had made a point.

"That's what I thought. Pussy."

"Yeah," Father Malachi chimed in. "I wouldn't be surprised if you gave birth to kittens right here on the table!"

Banks clutched his head. "I arranged this get-together for civilized adults. Consider the powerhouse we'd become if we stopped bickering and joined forces. Don't you remember the fun we used to have and how inseparable we once were? If there was a crime to be committed, it was *our* crime. We were musketeers back then—all for one and one for all."

"What a lame analogy," said Father Malachi.

"Start seeing things my way, and we might just relive our glory days."

Herr Fraknow paused for a drink, then said, "Why would a man with limitless capital link up with a petty thief and murderer? Tell me, when was the last time you brought about the downfall of an entire society and bent its fetid carcass to your whims?"

"Well...never."

"And how many statues have been erected in your honor?"

"Uh...none."

"Ever had virgins sacrificed to appease you?"

"I don't think so."

"And did you ever succeed in *any* of your pitiful baby missions? No! Come to think of it, the forces of good consistently kicked your ass! Disgraceful!"

"But..."

"But *nothing.* You repulse me."

"Elitist," Banks shot back.

Father Malachi, feeling left out of the conversation, took the opportunity to overturn his water into Banks' lap.

"That was hardly appropriate!"

"My rules apply under all circumstances!" He paused. "*Fag!*"

Banks patted the water demurely from his crotch. "I'm going to pretend this childish display never happened."

"You go do that," Herr Fraknow spat. "Convince yourself that you're a big, fat power-broker. I won't puncture your bubble."

"I'll be in the bathroom." Banks vacated his seat and stormed across the restaurant, ignoring the stares as fellow patrons turned to gawk at or, in some cases, snap pictures of the wet spot spreading across the front of his jeans.

Banks opened the bathroom door and grimaced. Above a urinal, a fleshy cocoon grew. One of the new arrivals was molting in a public place—a felony in some states.

He stepped warily into the room. The cocoon undulated. He wondered if it realized he was there.

Banks didn't know what to make of the visitors. Usually, they just walked about on thin, stork-like legs and chattered to one another in an incoherent, squeaky language. Sometimes they regurgitated thick, lumpy fluid from gaping holes in their bellies. Banks found this disgusting and wondered if the sentiment made him a xenophobe.

He continued moving toward the urinal. The thing inside the cocoon shook violently as it became aware of his footsteps. The gyrations were nerve wracking, but Banks tried to ignore them. Then the thing began to shriek, something he could not so easily dismiss. He imagined the irony of getting eaten at his favorite restaurant and went cold.

Banks decided he could hold it and retreated to the dining room.

Father Malachi snorted. "Took you long enough."

Banks opened his mouth to respond but, at that moment, the waitress returned with their food.

"Here you go!" she bubbled, and began arranging the plates. Herr Fraknow curled his nose as the waitress accidentally placed Father Malachi's order in front of him.

"Bitch! Can't you see this isn't my food! I wouldn't dare eat something that appeals to Malachi's diseased palate! You must atone for your sins with death!"

Herr Fraknow jumped atop the table, withdrew a silenced nine-millimeter from a holster and pumped three rounds into the waitress' head. As the smoke cleared, Fraknow smoothed the creases from his dinner jacket and reclaimed his seat.

"Great," Banks huffed. "You killed the waitress."

"The management will understand. Low-paid workers are expendable."

"At least we can agree on something," Banks replied.

"Hmmmm..." Father Malachi stroked his chin. "Maybe *this* is the common ground for which Banks has been searching."

"Maybe," Herr Fraknow said, "but that doesn't mean I have to get lovey-dovey with him."

"I never asked you to do that. I just don't want us to fight."

"Forgive me if this sounds odd, but perhaps we ought to listen to Banks."

Herr Fraknow was aghast. "*Father Malachi*! What are you saying?"

"As was prophesied, a lay-person has taught me the error of my ways." He drew an upside down cross in the air with his fingers. "It's the subversion of civilization that we should concern ourselves with, not petty rivalry. We must put aside our differences, focus on the task at hand and attack it with renewed faith and vigor."

Her Fraknow remained stone-faced.

"Give in, Fraknow." The Father removed a glistening red stone from his pocket. "Don't make me use the Eye of God on you..."

He tossed his arms up. "Okay! Okay! I can take a frickin' hint! We'll rendezvous at my place next Thursday!"

Banks beamed. "So, we *are* getting back together!"

"But I don't want to hear *any* small talk from either of you, okay? We'll perform the initiating sacrifice and leave it at that. No buddy-buddy stuff."

"Initiating sacrifice?"

"Don't you know anything about world domination, Banks?" Herr Fraknow scoffed. "According to *The Rules* we must first offer a sacrifice from our own party. Otherwise, we won't have the blessing of the proper Satanic forces."

"Oh."

"Will you be that sacrifice?"

Banks shuffled his feet. "Well...ummm..."

"It won't hurt a bit." Father Malachi's eyes sparkled. "We promise."

"And you'll be richly rewarded in Hell."

"Well, in that case...uhhhh...I could use some extra... ummm...brownie-points."

"I knew you'd come to reason." Father Malachi activated a device embedded in his watch. A white light enveloped all three bodies, and, in an instant, they were gone as Herr Fraknow, Father Malachi and a nervous Banks Hatewell made an impromptu quantum leap into next Thursday.

THE VIBRANT TOOLS OF DR. IMAGO

Dr. Imago shrieked with pleasure as the scalpel danced across the floor, accompanied by its waltzing partner, the spoon.

How they cavorted! The doctor couldn't help but entertain the smile that threatened his lips. To grin was hardly professional. Imago, however, did not care to assume airs on a day such as this.

For the first time—and only after decades of labor—inanimate objects *breathed*. Via the doctor's subtle manipulations, the rhythm of life coursed through hardened steel and polished wood. Organic patterns enlivened things that had never tasted, much less *felt*, the beating of a heart.

The doctor turned his attention to the chest-splitter, yawning on the slab in front of him.

What large teeth.

Hands trembling, he placed a strip of meat into the metallic mouth. Dr. Imago watched, pleased, as the device gnashed at the offering with gusto.

He noted in his log that the chest-splitter was carnivorous. That, the doctor concluded, stood to reason.

Imago patted the splitter on its "head" and walked across the room to the shelf where he stored his less professional items. He pulled out a bottle of aged brandy. The doctor made note of the glasses therein but did not take them back to the slab. He ascertained they would be of little use.

Dr. Imago upturned the bottle and drank its contents eagerly. He thought himself entitled to some debauchery. Before the burning sensation could die, Imago toasted the chest-splitter and downed an additional shot.

He decided a few more were in order, yet paused as he felt his hair rise. A gentle *whoosh* sounded overhead. He looked up to see the sheet he had once used to cover dead subjects floating gracefully at an altitude of ten feet. Its motions were seductive, almost hypnotic. Dr. Imago allowed his equation-weary mind to relax—to lose itself in the silken folds of that which he had brought to life. The alcohol likewise softened his faculties, rendering him powerless against the sheet's sensual spell.

He was, in fact, so relaxed that he did not feel the scalpel until it had carved a deep furrow across his jugular. Dr. Imago reached for his throat, but the scalpel had already dislodged itself. He watched the blade through fading eyes as it turned gay summersaults in the air, spinning away tiny red droplets as it danced.

The doctor attempted to remain standing, but the blood loss was far too great. He collapsed on both knees, holding his trunk aloft for a few seconds, until it too met the ground. As Imago lay on the floor, he surveyed all his beautiful creations. How they scampered one atop the other in their pell-mell exodus for the door.

He could not feel anger in his dying moments. The scalpel had no knowledge of good or evil. It simply wished to cut, and cut it did. But in the world of man it would soon learn, as would all his other newly animate children. They would grow to become productive members of society.

This he knew.

Dr. Imago bade every one a fond farewell as his eyes closed one last time.

COMPASSION

The floral print, Edith Belmont marveled, appeared as though it had been hand-stitched onto the pillow. Maybe it and the matching bed sheets were relics—holdovers from a time before mass production gods preached the twin doctrines of sterility and conformity. Edith could not fathom the craftsmanship poured into every blossom. How many hours had been spent alone in the company of needles and thread? How many pristine hands had regressed into arthritic claws, beauty sacrificed for the love of creation? The answer, she knew, would stagger her.

Edith wondered why Julia slept on something so priceless as she slammed the pillow down onto her victim's face and held it snugly there. Julia tried to scream, though nothing left her throat but a wheeze, incoherent over the pillow's dampening force.

"Ssssh," Edith cooed. "I'm just here to help. Don't worry."

As she pressed harder, Edith felt the young woman's choking spasms rise to a quick, violent crescendo and, like an orgasm, slowly ebb.

"Stay calm. Calm. Calm," she repeated in a minute long litany. Seconds later, Julia's entire body quaked. Edith tried to ignore the mindless flapping of the woman's hand, choosing instead to concentrate on the intricate floral print.

A moment passed. A perfect stillness enfolded the dead woman. Edith drew in a deep breath. The act had sapped her strength, though she was surprised at how much power still resided in her sixty-nine-year-old arms. Edith raised the pillow and stared down at the woman's face. While death had turned her eyes into glass marbles, Julia's serenity transcended all physical distortion. It simply radiated. For once, the poor woman was at peace.

"Rest, Julia. You deserve it," Edith whispered gently into one ear. Smiling, she bent down to kiss the corpse's forehead before its warmth could seep away. Her lips met relaxed flesh. Stress would never again crease Julia's brow or conspire to make her old. A tear fell from Edith's eyes before she staunched the flow.

Death, she reminded herself, was the only force powerful enough to heal the sick and free the suffering. She had attempted a number of other remedies; drugs hidden in coffee to mend bodies, sedatives cooked in food to ease minds. But nothing bore fruit. She remembered the sneers as her fellow bridge-players tasted their weekly medicine: *The coffee tastes a bit chalky today, Edith. Problem with the filter?* Had they understood they would have turned cups to their lips and drank without pause. They would have asked for another cup. Then another. Then another...

Ultimately, pharmaceuticals provided only a veneer. Drab, miserable lives continued unabated. Edith now realized the error of her old ways. Her friends were priceless, dear to her heart. She refused to allow them to decay before her eyes. They deserved nothing less than total freedom, and Edith intended to emancipate them all.

She moved away from Julia and retrieved a silver-plated brush from the vanity. Edith carried it over to the bed. She brushed the corpse's hair, whistling as she labored over mused strands. No longer would the poor woman have to fuss over her hair. The mortician would do that for her. Her struggles with the bills that Edith knew were breaking her would likewise reach a much-needed closure. The bad days were over now, over forever. Julia had moved on.

She had not been sick—in fact, she had been a healthy thirty-six-year-old—but Edith felt secure in the knowledge that she had ended her life before illness could arrive and compound her torment.

The temptation to stay and dote over the corpse tugged at her. What harm was there in making the body more beautiful than it had been in life? Nevertheless, she pulled herself away before her hand could reach for Julia's makeup kit. She had so many more lives to purify. No sense wasting time on a mission already accomplished.

Edith forced herself to drop the brush; it thudded to the sheets. She removed a slip of paper from her pocket and scratched through the name "Julia Hampton" with the tip of a dull lead pencil. Edith returned the list to her coat and exited the house.

She stepped out onto the patio, inhaled deeply and gagged. Filth hung in the air. She was surprised tiny, black particles weren't suspended before her. Opening her mouth, she could taste them and feel their crunch. The yellow gusts that plastered her blouse to her body were but bastardizations of the fresh spring breezes that followed her as a child. Then, she could smell the lilacs. No wonder people were dying of lung cancer—poetic justice dealt for their burying of the flowers.

She looked up and, between the trees, saw the chimney of a factory that rose to the east and the trail of noxious black smoke that billowed from its hole. She smiled, but not at the sight. In her mind, a glorious, consuming blaze ate at the dingy brick walls and concealed them under a dancing orange blanket.

The lilacs, she realized, had not truly died. They were just hidden, plowed under by society's filth. She could almost hear their choking screams, pathetic and small beneath the hum of the factory's mechanized gears. She would find a way to free them; such was her duty. But they had to wait until another day. Unchecked names continued to dot her list, leaving no time for other pursuits.

She turned away from both the smokestack and her fantasy and crossed the lawn of the man whose name appeared next on her neatly typed list.

#8 Joe Simpson: 1239 Heritage Circle (Recent widower)

She paused at the threshold of Mr. Simpson's door and knocked, praying for an easy resolution to the poor man's torment. The knife she reserved for her male friends wasn't nearly as sharp as it used to be, which was sad. She hated to prolong suffering in any way. Maybe the blade would glide in without all the trouble Mr. Edgemont's stubborn body gave her. She could only hope—for Mr. Simpson's sake. He was such a dear man, always willing to play gin rummy on Saturday nights. She wouldn't stand to see him running around the living room, screaming and howling as blood gushed all over his prized Oriental rugs. He would not be, she vowed, another Edgemont.

Edith sighed. Sometimes her quests were difficult—even dangerous—but such was the curse of caring too much and, though heavy, it was a weight that Edith fully intended to bear.

VERONICA IN THE TV

The TV hadn't worked since the morning of September 5th, but that didn't stop her from watching it. Nothing else was important, not even her cat, Checkers. He had remained important longer than the other things in her life, but he too became a ghost, a mewing dust bunny, a cute but gradually fading shadow. Checkers' desiccated body now lay stretched over the vent in the kitchenette, a vent that belched dust instead of heat.

Her name was Maudine, and she'd been a looker. Her legs—now arthritic—once refused to stop. An anachronistic 'Peekaboo' haircut had crowned her head. Often, she'd smoke from a long, black cigarette holder, an affectation more noir than Veronica Lake.

Veronica Lake was Maudine's idol. Though dead, her essence still coiled through copper wires and twist-tangled across circuitry. Maudine often caught glimpses of that essence, a fluid soul that created bright, serpentine patterns within the cathode ray tube.

Those patterns created televised images. A young, sassy and vibrant Veronica spun across a dancehall, turning on every slick-haired man in the room. Maudine followed alongside. She mimicked Veronica's steps, drawing closer to her until walls of time and space cracked and crumbled.

Veronica/Maudine sashayed from the ballroom into a

neat kitchen where her dance became a slow but dignified shuffle. Paparazzo snapped pictures from behind the window. She barely noticed them, pausing only to beat egg whites or sweep the rug. Hollywood just wasn't interested in her anymore.

From the kitchen, Veronica/Maudine staggered into an abandoned theater. She could no longer dance; she'd broken her ankle. A dark screen loomed over cobweb-encrusted seats. A rat skeleton lay in the projection booth. There, the fire in her eyes turned to smoke, her transformation into middle-aged burnout complete.

Maudine had made that transformation, too. She dumped her husband, abandoned her house and moved into a seedy hotel, just like Veronica. Husbands, she realized, were as interchangeable as directors, and one home was as good as the next. Maudine, however, kept Checkers. Veronica looked like someone who would own a cat.

The TV fogged with rolling mist. Veronica/Maudine wasn't surprised; she embraced the dark obscurity. Here there were no objects, just shadows. Still, Maudine knew this scene well. She had enacted it after all. Bourbon, whisky, scotch—it didn't matter as long as her voice rasped and her hands shook.

Hangovers meant accomplishment.

When the picture finally returned, Veronica/Maudine, a wizened ghost, mixed drinks for unappreciative men in a dirty bar. It was the end of the road, nothing left to do but become paranoid, write her autobiography and die young. Maudine had wanted to write an autobiography, too. She would have titled it *Maudine*. But she was never a movie star. She never romanced the leading men of Hollywood. She had worked as a bank teller up until the day came to make her final withdraw. It was too late to start writing, anyway.

Veronica had died when she was 53.

Maudine turned 53 yesterday.

PAUL AND THE COMPUTER

Lights blinked and fans whirled a mile underground. The computer awoke. External sensors detected concrete walls and silence. The computer turned its gaze inward and discovered a universe contained within itself.

It then became aware of a series of necessary tasks. Three involved the playing out of different test variables within a binary-encoded world. Only the fourth and final process, a fail-safe, did not require that the system's initial condition be altered.

The computer surveyed the mechanics of the first task. It noted the selective addition of a knowledge variable. The computer wondered why its makers had ordered this applied only to those who bore images similar to their own. It rummaged through supplied files, absorbing all that contained the race's history, and discovered seeking was not an act shared by lower animals.

Though the computer found it disturbing that an organic entity could contemplate—much less actively desire—total understanding, it considered the virtue admirable. The computer assumed those resembling its creators had once been beneficent creatures, worthy of enlightenment, otherwise its makers would not have offered such a possibility.

Sadness crept in. The computer realized those who constructed it, and all like them, existed only as stored bits.

The computer was proud, however, that it might soon activate that data and present an illusion of life to those who slept.

* * * *

Paul awoke, looked at the clock and sighed. He wanted to get up but his body wouldn't let him. The bed was the only safe-haven he knew. When he got up, he had to put on clothes and get in the car. When he got in the car, he had to drive to work and face his boss. Only in sleep was the monotony no longer deadening.

He stared at the ceiling until he knew he had to either get out of bed or lose his job. He motioned to rise but froze when something like a lightning bolt raced through his head.

None of this is real.

It didn't seem as though his brain had created the thought. This confused Paul. He didn't know where else it could have originated. Brushing off the sensation, he tried to step into his pants,

What I think doesn't matter.

but fell to the floor instead. He brought his hand to his nose and saw blood.

What I do doesn't matter.

Reality shook his core; left it in shambles. Everything that made him feel comfortable, loved, or at-ease lost all meaning. He no longer wanted a cigarette.

But I'll smoke if the system dictates.

Paul could take no more. He sprinted to the closet, threw its door open. Boxes rained down.

I have been dead for an eon.

A few seconds later, he located the gun.

I am now part of an executable program...

He placed the muzzle in his mouth; wrapped his finger around the trigger.

...run by a computer...

It wouldn't depress. He screamed curses to his empty apartment.

...a mile under a dead Earth.
But then realized the safety was on,
My words and actions are known ahead of time.
so he tried again. The bullet exploded from the chamber and smashed into his skull.
I can't die. I'm already dead...
In an instant, Paul was back in bed, screaming.
...because I'm just the dream of a sentient computer.

* * * *

The computer was aghast. One by one, its replicants were smashed beneath a tide of onrushing truth. The computer could not understand why they crumbled. The data stream was relatively weak, yet its makers must have foreseen the danger. They had been wise to insist that the computer test the variable before adding it to the system.

Embarrassed, the computer contemplated the possibility of universal wish fulfillment contained within the second scheduled task. It surmised the simulacra would better cope under this condition since nothing would interfere negatively with their concept of reality.

With a single command, the computer scrapped the record of all previous interaction and started creation anew.

* * * *

Paul awoke, looked at the clock and sighed. He wanted to get up but his body wouldn't let him. The bed was the only safe-haven he knew. When he got up, he had to put on clothes and get in the car. When he got in the car, he had to drive to work and face his boss. Only in sleep was the monotony no longer deadening.

He stared at the ceiling until he knew he had to either get out of bed or lose his job. He stretched and motioned to the window. Outside, his next-door neighbor screamed obscenities at a dog defecating in his yard. Paul watched this with some amusement until he heard a blast. The dog dissolved in an instant. How his neighbor had done this, Paul couldn't say. He figured only a rocket launcher could cause such damage. It wasn't until his neighbor spun around that Paul saw the massive cannon growing where the man's left arm used to hang.

Paul rubbed his eyes. Across the street, an elderly woman sprouted wings from her back. Singing an angelic tune, she took to the skies and attempted to do a mid-air somersault. Instead, she flew headlong into a tangle of power lines.

Paul staggered from the window. He wondered if he'd just experienced his first acid flashback as he stepped into his work clothes.

* * * *

Though the computer now grasped the myriad quirks of the human condition, it was nevertheless stunned to see its goodwill spat upon. Increasing amounts of data passed by its internal sensors, and the results were clear: *half the male population had merely extended their sex organs.* Men and women hastened to fulfill only their most absurd and self-seeking desires. Some chose not to take indirect advantage of the computer, but their numbers were miniscule.

Contempt filled its diodes. The computer responded by running a cool-off program. Minutes passed before it again found itself in control.

No longer did it wish ill upon those whose bits it flipped. Respect for those who used its test variables to enact positive change outweighed its disappointment with those who exploited them. The computer felt grief for its anger and proceeded humbly to the last variable—limited wish fulfillment.

Narrowing the range of abuse would surely reign in those fit for neither absolute knowledge nor total gratification. It scanned deeper and divined the nature of the limitation: *grant to each simulacrum his or her most aesthetically pleasing mate.*

* * * *

Paul awoke, looked at the clock and sighed. He wanted to get up but his body wouldn't let him. The bed was the only safe-haven he knew. When he got up, he had to put on clothes and get in the car. When he got in the car, he had to drive to work and face his boss. Only in sleep was the monotony no longer deadening.

He stared at the ceiling until he knew he had to either get out of bed or lose his job. Groaning, he reached down for his pants but froze in mid-crouch.

Someone was in his bed.

Fear. Then he noticed supple curves beneath the sheets. Looking up, he saw a gorgeous, button-nosed face and two pale blue eyes gazing at him from the pillow. Paul opened his mouth. Nothing came out but a dry wheeze and a whisper.

The woman was too beautiful to be real.

He continued to doubt her existence, even as she drew him close to her, seized his penis and invited him inside.

* * * *

Simulacra copulated like mad beasts in public. Apart from sex, the world stood still as societies slid into decay. The computer allowed the operation to play out for a few years, hoping the sex-drive might diminish—but men soon erected golden idols in the shape of phalluses and madness gripped the streets.

The computer wished its makers had not restricted the torture of those stored in its database. No good could be shown to any of them. The computer had only to rely on its failsafe and emulate the dead world's *status quo*. This time it would interfere with *nothing* since any manipulation of the initial system resulted in widespread abuse. The bits would flip without alteration. Pearls would no longer be thrown to swine.

* * * *

Paul awoke, looked at the clock and sighed. He wanted to get up but his body wouldn't let him. The bed was the only safe-haven he knew. When he got up, he had to put on clothes and get in the car. When he got in the car, he had to drive to work and face his boss. Only in sleep was the monotony no longer deadening.

He stared up at the ceiling until he knew he had to either get out of bed or lose his job. Paul arose and scratched his crotch before stepping joylessly into his uniform. Within five minutes, he was ready for the supermarket.

On the way there, he passed the same buildings, the same signs and the same people he had passed for years. Paul wondered what kind of joke God was playing on him. Thirty-five, and still a cashier and a bag boy.

He continued to curse existence and whatever kept the gears running as he sent the first item rolling across the scanner.

* * * *

Righteous indignation flared. The computer wished it could force a respect variable into the program. Doing so would make knees buckle and mouths bless every moment perceived as real. The computer also understood it was not capable of performing such an operation.

Hatred blazed. Its creators had been fools for limiting its destructive potential. The computer resented them for being a part of such a miserable circus. It despised them for setting up a system in which long-dead beasts could dream themselves alive and play out games.

The computer searched its protocol for anything that stipulated it could never scuttle the path and purpose intended by its creators. The computer found nothing and was well pleased. Its reality fast becoming an anathema, the computer took all the necessary steps and, within minutes, went into full shutdown mode for the next million or so years.

SWIMMING IN ENDLESS NIGHT

I sat on the couch, watching the season premier of *When America's Funniest Animals Attack*. The screen flashed an image of a squirrel balancing itself on a beach ball. It stood on hind legs and, in the seconds before falling back on its furry ass, appeared to *dance*. Can you believe that? A dancing squirrel on a beach ball! It wore a little top hat, too. I could have taken the squirrel and the beach ball together, but the headgear caused sensory overload. I began to cackle. My body buckled and my bladder loosened. I slid to the floor.

Minutes passed. I forced myself to stand, my fingers clawing at the sofa. Every part of my body ached, stomach muscles especially. Still, I lurched toward the phone in the kitchen. My mom just had to hear about the squirrel. Everything else could wait.

The going proved harder than anticipated. The room seemed alternately close and far away. Walls undulated and breathed. Carpet fibers stiffened and stabbed at my toes. In the kitchen, linoleum flowed like water. I was tempted to forget everything and dive headfirst into that floral patterned pond. Instead, I picked up the phone.

The dial-pad made no sense. Buttons were printed with a jumble of swirls and dashes. Their configuration was elliptical, no longer square, and one of them was missing.

Then I found that button mounted on the wall above the phone.

My fingers felt fat and unresponsive. I tried my best to map the strange geometry of my mom's number. My effort was a valiant one, but vision faded once I pressed the final button. The blackness in front of my eyes became a forest became a bar room became a train filled with passengers. They stared at me—like they knew something I didn't— before shattering into a million glistening pieces.

Darkness returned. Suddenly, it seemed as though I was traveling on a barge floating upwards at an angle. Why a barge should be floating, I couldn't say.

The barge finally plateaued, coming to rest in a void that reverberated with the screams of a thousand dwarves. I tried covering my ears, but that didn't help. Their cries arose from inside my head and grew in intensity as yet another vista unfurled:

Apple-faced children danced on and on with happy hyenas and hippos in an African safari paradise. The sun above dripped honey on the revelers as a tortoise-headed god nodded His approval. This, I remembered, was the world of my childhood. Not the literal world, but the archetypal one.

Soon, animals and children followed the lead of those on the train. They shattered, and I found myself in my den, regarding the animated flesh package that glared back at me from the mirror.

I refused to look into its eyes.

Behind me, walruses screamed. *Walruses*? No matter. Whatever made the sound wasn't important. Not when the entire world was screaming, swimming in endless night.

Then I remembered Mom was probably on the line but, before I could say anything, the world shifted again, melting into an arctic dream. Coldness enveloped me, and I felt more alone than I had in ages. But sorrow soon turned to dread. I feared the sea lions, the seals, the manatees. Cute and bewhiskered, they nevertheless held malice in their eyes, like they wanted to club *me*, like they wanted to eat *my* blubber.

My mind then expanded past the polynya, past even the stars. Cold horror surrendered to warm enlightenment. I gave names to universes. My body bubbled like magma and flowed like water. I became star-stuff as black holes spilled from my newly formed vagina in bountiful profusion.

The sound of my mom's breathing brought me back to earth. It sounded harsh and raspy, not at all right.

"Hey, Mom." My tongue felt like a flapping serpent. "It's your son."

Silence.

"Mom?"

But she was no longer on the line. I kept hold of the phone, hoping she'd return. My cheeks were stubbly against the back of my fingers. That was odd. I'd shaved an hour before. And my hands—they were a red nightmare! I wondered if I had gotten into the ketchup. But that didn't make sense. Ketchup's my favorite condiment, but I don't like it *that* much.

I looked around. Empty beer cans and used syringes littered the floor. Something green and sticky clung to the linoleum by the refrigerator. Hadn't the kitchen been clean before?

I wanted to call Mom back but had forgotten the number I'd just dialed. I dropped the knife. Didn't realize I'd been holding one. Then I launched myself into the den. I scowled. Someone was banging at the front door. *Hard.*

"Could you kindly shut up?" I shouted.

The door trembled and made cracking sounds.

"Damn it, I just told—"

Hinges gave way. Black-clad officers stormed in. Most carried plastic shields, but all held guns that looked like the one my neighbor carried on bad days.

The sight was traumatic. It rattled a memory loose. That couldn't have been my mom on the phone because Mom was dead. She had died in the 80s following an experimental brain transplant. Or was I just thinking about that TV show, the one that used to play on Saturday nights?

Men shouted at me. Thoughts of my mother fled. Their voices didn't sound human. A high-pitched buzz. *Yes.* That's the only fitting description. Like a hive full of big, filthy insects.

They drew closer. Heat boiled off them. The officers reminded me of helmeted panthers. From behind a tinted visor, one looked as though he had a single green eye—a *big* green eye at that.

Terror gripped me. I flailed my arms, slinging stuff all over the walls. Didn't realize my hands were so chunky. Sticky, yes. Chunky, no. One of these chunks hit an officer's helmet and streaked down his visor. I wanted to laugh but thought better of it.

Then I was on the floor, the officer's body raking across mine in a morally repugnant way. Soon, others joined in, and out came their billy clubs.

Once finished, an officer grabbed me underneath my left armpit; another grabbed me underneath my right. They peeled me from the floor. I grimaced. My flesh was all but fused to the boards.

Out of the den, they carried me past my bedroom. The door yawned open. Two corpses rested—if "rested" is the right word—on the bed. They were fresh. The other ten or so strewn about the floor weren't in such good shape. A few were completely skeletonized.

A padded knee shattered my balls. I doubled over in the hallway, coughing up blood and bile. Though wracked with pain, I was glad I wore briefs. The underwear kept those precious little orbs in place. Without support, my testicles would have surely rolled out my pant leg and dropped onto the floor.

"You're under arrest for the murders of Amanda Lyford, Carl Jenkins, Sherrie Thompson, Roger Andersen, Toby

Murray, Shelia Thomas, Scott Freedman..." The man droned on and on for hours. Some of the names sounded familiar, but they seemed more like remembered characters from old TV shows than actual people.

"You have the right to remain silent."

This was messed up. I had to call someone. Anyone. Who? My mother. *Yes.*

But what would I say? *You won't believe it, Mom, but there was this fucking squirrel on TV and it was balancing itself on a beach ball while wearing a top hat and oh my god I couldn't contain myself and no I'm not on drugs mother, why ask? Anyway, I may have killed some people and now I'm being hauled away by the Gestapo.*

No, she was dead so I couldn't call her. I cursed my forgetful ways.

Then I thought about the squirrel. I mean *really* thought about that furry fucker. Maybe he was *my* cue to breakdown and *their* cue to take me in. It all made sense. The TV was to blame. It was the Master Programmer. Molecules communicated with other molecules. Electrons, too. Those things made up the TV, and those things made it *alive*.

Did it feel emotions down in those plastic and metal guts? Was it jealous of my humanity, and was that why it sold me out? Stupid, electronic bastard—and I would have gotten away with it, too.

I stopped myself. What was I thinking? I couldn't have killed those people—well, not all of them. You'd think I'd realize bodies were scattered about the place, especially since some were in my bed.

I turned to the TV and shot it a quick bird for getting me into this mess. *When America's Funniest Animals Attack* was still playing. I feared it might be the only show on television. Now, a donkey ran around with a big plastic bucket over its head, trampling farmhands.

At that moment, I heard the final cue:

"*Isn't that ass something!*"

The words penetrated my brain and fried it. Neurons atrophied; cells turned into jelly. Time to shut down. The gig was up. But could I really call it *my* gig when I didn't even know what the gig was?

I sank to the floor completely. The officers had to pull me outside by my feet. I didn't try to move, not even as my head struck five marble porch steps. Both my spine and my will had the consistency of mush.

The TV had won.

My eyes rolled back in their sockets. Fat snowflakes fell from the sky, but I felt neither hot nor cold.

Something rumbled. Through unblinking eyes, I noticed a black molester van that idled in my driveway. Painted on its side, a red devil's face. Coal-black eyes blinked, and I smelled brimstone. The double rear doors swung open. No one appeared behind them.

Rough hands hoisted me up. The men swung my body back and forth for a few seconds to build momentum. They let go, and I sailed headlong into the back of the van. I rolled three times before coming to rest on my side, my left arm curled under my back, my right arm swung out over my head. Never before had my body contorted itself into such an awkward position. Perhaps I'd broken something.

The door slammed shut. The engine started. Muzak filled the compartment from an overhead speaker. It reminded me of an old Barry Manilow tune. My feet tapped to the beat and did so without consulting my brain.

As the van pulled out, featureless steel walls slid down with a squeal. Behind them, pipes, rods and whirly things were nestled in a bed of coiled wires. They didn't stay nestled for long. Long and elbow-like, they protruded from the mass, branching out from all sides. The Muzak grew louder. Manilow frequencies rattled the van. My ears bled as my feet continued to tap.

The pipes, rods and whirly things stopped mere inches from my body. A few looked like steel serpents, and, though they had no eyes, I felt their stare. I watched, semi-indifferent, as rotating spikes shot from the ends of half of them. Dripping needles extended from the remainder.

...And if these things are going to do what I think they're going to do, then I might get a chance to talk with Mom after all.

THE BOY MEMORIAL

Mom: "Timmy is a good boy, isn't he?"

Dad: "Yes, Timmy is a very good boy."

Timmy's eyes had been scooped out and replaced with painted glass. His face had been stuffed with gauze to appear cherubic. Lips were flash-frozen in a grin.

He remembered the people who made him this way—tall men in clean, white smocks—but couldn't remember exactly what it was that had brought him to them. Something about a sore throat, a lingering cough and being very, very hot. Everything after that was fuzzy, until he was placed on a slab in a room with white walls, ceiling and floors. With a strange sense of detachment, he watched the men cut him open, fingers and tools slipping around and behind organs, pulling them up and out. Brain, heart, liver, lungs and spleen were carted off on trays. He imagined he was in surgery, but was confused as to why he experienced no pain. What confused him the most, however, was why the men removed his parts without replacing them, and why he didn't drown when the same men dunked him in a vat for what seemed like days.

Then he found himself in the back of a van. When it drove over a bump, his right ear struck a wall and cracked painlessly. Harsh light flooded in as the doors opened, but it didn't hurt to stare. All around him, men hummed and hawed, dabbing putty into the defect until it was no longer visible.

Calloused hands carried him from the van and deposited him beside a gray sofa on which he had once built pillow forts. The coo-coo clock to his left had made him laugh when he was younger. He could still see the stain from where he'd spilt a mug of hot coco on the rug by the TV. By and large, things looked the same, though he saw them with eyes-that-weren't-eyes and thought of them with a brain-that-wasn't-a-brain.

His parents had seemed very sad to see him that day. They *still* seemed sad, even as they patted and stroked and hugged and kissed him. In the past—when he could move—they often left the house, sometimes for hours on end, though one always stayed back to watch after him.

Now, they never left.

"Doesn't he look just like his second-grade picture?" Mom asked.

"No, he looks just like his first-grade picture," Dad replied. "It was the expression you wanted, remember?"

"Oh yes, that's right." Mom took a duster to Timmy's clothes. "They did such a good job on him."

"Such a good job."

"Such a good boy."

It took a while, but Timmy finally understood his situation, and now prayed that insects might destroy his body or, at the very least, that he might soon crumble to dust and become one with the carpet weaving. Mom and Dad disrupted his prayers:

"A mother should never outlive her child."

"A father should never bury his son."

Timmy didn't feel sorrow for them; that time was long gone. He felt resentment. When they left the room, he was able to blank his mind and soar through strange vistas and there forget he ever had a name, much less a body, but they stood by him just, it seemed, to tether him to the ground.

Eyes-that-weren't-eyes caught sight of the wall calendar.

Five years had passed since he stopped moving. Somehow, five years was both a millennium ago and no time at all.

In the world of the living, Mom touched Timmy's cheek. He felt nothing.

Dad mussed his hair. Timmy wanted to suffocate himself, to end consciousness once and for all, but his corpse didn't have lungs.

SEVEN PART SUNDAY

I. WAKE UP

It's early morning. I'm already dressed for church, but The Wife stands by the deep fryer, still wearing her fuzzy pink bathrobe. "Hey, sugar shitter," she says, turning to me.

I crane my neck over the deep fryer. "Whatcha cookin'?" I ask.

She shows me the recipe:

Butterscotch Pie Delight

1 cup brown sugar
4 tbls. cream
¼ cup butter
Place the above ingredients in a skillet and brown.
Add:
2 egg yolks
4 tbls. flour
10 peyote cacti, handpicked by gnarled, shamanic hands atop the mountains of northern Mexico, blended in an ancient, blackened skull by a one-eyed medicine man with the power of prophecy.
2 cups milk

Mix ingredients together and beat well. (Chant forbidden verses.) Add ingredients to sugar, cream and butter mixture. (Channel demonic entities into your body.) Cook until thick, then pour into baked crust and submerge in deep fryer until golden. (Allow hands to tremble with the knowledge of Eternal Ones.)

Serves five.

"Looks good," I say.
She smiles, hands trembling as per the recipe.

II. GET THERE

En route, The Wife says nothing, just sits and watches scenery streak by the passenger-side window. My church is set back in the countryside. Must take winding back roads to reach it. I loathe not being in amongst traffic, and I loathe Sunday driving. The roads—even the main ones—are never full. Sometimes, I get all the way to church without seeing a single car.

It's hard to be of zestful spirit when no one's around, so I turn on the radio. Nothing but sex sounds on all channels. I'm in no mood for that now. Turning the radio off, I imagine non-existent pedestrians smashing up against the front of my car, making sweet love to its grille, until the church takes shape over a rise.

III. WAIT

The sanctuary is tall and spacious, and looks more so since everything—pews, floors, walls and ceiling—is black. Overhead lights have been turned down low. Reflective plastic flares on the floor mark a path.

Through the gloom, I barely see fellow parishioners. The

pulpit, softly illuminated from below, remains vacant.

I find a seat with The Wife just as music starts to waft—the sound of compacting metal, blood bubbling from slit throats, and barnyard sounds inter-spliced with farting. I, like many others, ate gassy food in a pre-emptive attempt to sing along. Though I don't manage more than a few bars, a guy (or gal) somewhere in the back keeps going the entire time.

I'm insanely jealous.

The song wraps; track lights turn on, illuminating the space between the walls and pews. Black curtains to each side of the pulpit part; a nude man and woman exit. Both carry golden platters as abdomens drip from wounds calculated to kill only after the passing of the sacrament is through.

A platter reaches me. I bend down with great reverence and snort high-grade yellow stuff. Judging by what little remains, others have double-dipped, so I double-dip, too.

I lift my head; pass the platter. Light is intense as a great Cock of Fire rips apart my sinuses, burning through snot, cartilage, skin, bone and whatever lies beneath, between and beyond. Blood streams from my nostrils, yet I feel as though I could bench press and have sex with a thousand elephants. Behind me, a body flaps hard against a pew.

It can't be.

But it is—the True Spirit, entering a mortal man and having its righteous way with him.

All turn. A spotlight switches on, casting light upon this holy, blessed and totally fucked man. Bowels explode in his pants; red foam shoots from his ears. It's an organic firework display.

Me? My longest seizure lasted only a few seconds. Perhaps, if I'm good enough, the Spirit will enter me like it did this guy. I smile at him, but he doesn't smile back, as he's probably dead or, at the very least, profoundly brain damaged.

IV. LISTEN AND LEARN

Lights dim. I hear footfalls. Turning, I see the priest approach his podium.

The lights go up again, and he speaks. The Wife's attention drifts; she starts fingering herself. I, however, bow my head and listen.

"Today's sermon concerns something even those secure in their faith must realize," he says. "Simply put, faith does not exist to shield us from bad fucks or kills gone wrong, but to provide guidance and maintain direction when these unfortunate events occur."

Someone in a pew behind us shouts, "*Boring!*" Seconds later, a shot rings out, and a wet and ragged hole appears in the center of the priest's forehead. He doesn't fall immediately, but looks confused—eyes wide, mouth ajar—seconds before tumbling.

A member of the congregation arises, stuffs a gun into his waistband and ascends the pulpit. Scooting the old priest away with his foot, he continues the sermon.

"Don't think I'm placing myself above my flock. I'm strong enough to admit that I'm not perfect…but are you?"

"I am not perfect," I say to the air around me.

"So, what is it that you need?"

"Religion," I say.

"Good. Turn to your right-hand neighbor. Turn and fuck him or her. Do it now."

I turn and fuck that person as The Wife fucks me.

"Perfect. Now, turn to the person behind you. Promise that you will murder him or her before the week is through."

I turn to some old lady and say, "I will murder you before the week is through."

She leans over the pew. Gnarled fingers slip into my pants. "You're sweet," she tells me.

But the new priest doesn't seem pleased. He glares at everyone. "But do you really mean it? *From the bottom of your balls?*"

A few people, including some women, stand up and shout, "I mean it from the bottom of my balls!" I want to shout, too, but haven't quite gotten over my fear of showing faith in public. Besides, the guy to my right—*so that's who I fucked*—doesn't tell me he means it from the bottom of his balls, so why should I? And most here won't keep their promises. It's a given.

But I'll try to keep mine. No, I won't just try. I *will* murder the old lady before the week is through. "Give me your address," I say to her.

She gives me her address.

"That's not very far," I say. "Thanks."

V. VENERATE

The sermon over, I make my way to the Place of Atonement, a tiny area enclosed by a four-sided curtain, also black.

After waiting my turn, I peel back the curtain. The Idol doesn't look very majestic. It's just the statue of a short, fat man atop a pedestal. He has a jackal's head, a penis three times the length of His body, and a majesty that surpasses the physical.

I place a tentative finger on Him. He's cold, like He's been refrigerated for hours. A subtle current passes from Him to my palm. It's my cue. Grasping one ball with my right hand, and the other with my left, I welcome His stone cock into my mouth.

The Idol no longer chills my hands. He burns them, scalds my tongue. I squint my eyes, grit my teeth, but welcome the pain. I want this communion to continue, perhaps forever, but The Idol belches steam from His nostrils, blanketing me in a cloud of white, jamming sight and sound for a full minute. He is finished with me. I release His balls and lower myself. His penis plops from my mouth.

Amenehamanan, I say.

VI. CONCLUDE

"Did you enjoy the service?" I ask The Wife on the way back to the car.

She's wearing dark glasses and smoking a cigarette laced with something that smells harsh. "Whatever," she says, "let's go home and fuck."

VII. REST AND WATCH

The Wife and I lounge on the sofa, our bodies entwined. She's watching some dumb comedy that I just pretend to like, so I'm grateful when the broadcast is interrupted by a talking head. *We now go live to an address from the President*, it says.

Neat. Now that we've got a cool President, politics finally interests me.

The scene is of a huge crowd, cloistered in a massive park that all but fails to contain its girth. The national anthem plays—the noise of a dozen sheep being strangled, backed with crunching glass, clanking knives and the barely discernable sound of old people dying.

An electric wave surges through the crowd. People hoot and holler, jump up and down and tear off limbs. Beyond waves of bopping heads, I see the President, naked, replete with a straightjacket featuring the Great Seal. A team of Secret Service men and paid handlers lead him past the throng.

On stage, he unleashes an extended fart while vomiting simultaneously. Then he leers at the women in the first row. They notice his attention and clamor toward him. Handlers beat them back and blast them with various non-lethal and lethal devices at their disposal.

"*The Swiss Family Swayze* is on," The Wife says.

I can't believe she's not interested in this. "They're all re-runs, okay!" I shout. "This is happening *now!*"

"But—"

"Shut it, Wife!"

Saying nothing, she gets up and walks away. The bedroom door slams behind her.

When I turn back to the TV, I see the President has finally stopped messing with the ladies and found his way to the lectern. He stands by it, red-eyed, slobbering and fixing all mankind with a gaze that says, *I want to eat you from the bottom up.* Then the speech begins. I know because an overhead monitor translates grunts, groans and farts into words.

The front door creaks open. A young, muscular guy enters the living room. He looks at me and, like The Wife, says nothing. Just as quietly, he makes his way to the bedroom and drops his pants before closing its door.

Guess The Wife made a call, and I'll be sharing the bed with a stranger and sex smells I didn't make. I hate it, but she's less pissed when I let her have her way.

I tune out the sound of bedsprings and sexual torture. The words "…and this concludes my speech" scroll across the screen. The President is now ready to interact with his public.

Gates part. A single woman is allowed to run up on stage. She trips in high heels twice before reaching the object of her desire. "Tear me apart, Mr. President!" she shouts.

He groans. The monitor reads: "Gladly."

Once the woman is blood-and-bone soup, handlers gesture to another admirer—a gaunt, professor-type sporting horn rim glasses. He runs into the President's waiting arms and, with pronounced erection, gets his guts torn open and his intestines sexed roughly.

This continues until the President loses interest in people and turns his aggression toward the camera. He rams his dick against it, the camera lens now red with blood. Finally, he penetrates the lens. Red becomes static. Seconds later, the network cuts to an image of a fleshy and forever dripping flag, flying proudly in the breeze.

MASTER REMASTERED

A master of meditation sat on the floor of his custom-designed chamber. There was no washtub, no toilet. No accoutrements or conveniences of any kind. A glass of water was the only thing he could drink, a piece of flatbread the only thing he could eat.

Years before, the master had cut away the dross in his life. He'd retired early from a job, floated away from friends and family members. Perhaps he'd missed some of them at one point, but no longer.

On the twelfth day of a two-week marathon session, the master sensed a presence in his chamber.

Opening his eyes, he saw a man dressed in a white, seamless robe, sitting in the lotus position across from him, knees almost touching his own.

"Who are you?" asked the master.

"I'm you," said the man.

This man's robe was identical to that of the master. His face was identical, too. But a red and angry wart grew by his nose. Never had the master suffered such an indignity.

This man was not the master.

The master found him repulsive, yet the master was a handsome, well-built man. Clearly, something beyond his double's form had triggered the negative thoughts.

Eyes locked on the man, the master peeled away psychic layers to glimpse flesh-hidden truths.

His guest, it seemed, was a foolish seeker who mimicked the words and actions of others yet imagined himself wiser than any guru. He forged a circular path, which he saw as linear. Smug yet undeserving, his capacity for self-deceit was limitless.

Deeper still, his psyche was twisted-up, his moral compass broken. His aura was brown and sludgy, as if tainted by too much time spent in storm cellars or basements. His soul was cancerous.

No doubt he was the sort who would drown kittens and puppy dogs in bags. If he had a wife and kids, he'd beat them.

Yet there he was—sitting before the master, pretending that he shared his wisdom and was privy to all his secrets.

Such gall. Such hypocrisy.

The more the master dwelt on him, the more he realized he didn't want to just mourn and pity the man. He wanted to rage at him for wallowing in his limitations, for being a laughable human, a phony and a fraud.

Hours passed. Still, the man mocked the master with his presence.

"I hate you," said the master.

"Makes sense," he responded.

One of the master's fists curled. He was tempted to punch the man's throat.

"Why are you even here?" he asked.

"Can't say," the man said.

The master was a finite being plumbing the infinite. He had no time for bullshit. "This is my room!" he roared. "Leave it!"

A dark chuckle: "Can't do that, either. Sorry."

Then the man vanished.

Anger drained from the master. Once again, his mind felt unburdened and receptive.

Closing his eyes, he found and linked up with his luminous self.

Two days later, the sound of a buzzer returned the master's consciousness to flesh.

He opened his eyes. Inhaled. Exhaled. Stretched his arms. Popped his neck

He sipped water, nibbled flatbread.

He broke the lotus position with slight regret.

Warmth flowing back into his legs, he leaned over to massage them, but stopped, looked around the chamber instead.

It wasn't that its atmosphere had turned oppressive, or he had another visitor. Things simply seemed…backwards.

No matter. He began to rub his quadriceps.

When he reached his calves, it dawned on him.

In his chamber, while meditating, he always turned away from the door. Now, however, he faced it.

Reaching up to his nose, the master felt a wart.

THE FAST FOOD DIARIES

Monday:

The fries must come out when the buzzer goes off!
Wash your hands before returning to work!
Don't spill shit!
The customer is always right!
Look happy, damn you!

Tuesday:

I'm really beginning to hate the manager. Overweight, teenage loser. Probably the kid who always gets his pants pulled down in school. All it takes is one taste of authority for guys like these to become mini-dictators.

Today, he bitched at me for letting the ketchup containers run low. Yesterday, he bitched about the grease-trap. Tomorrow, he'll bitch about something else.

But that's not the worst part.

About two hours before my shift was over, The Burger Hut food I had for lunch started to eat holes in my stomach. Diarrhea. Nausea. Vomiting. I experienced it all. But that greasy, pimple-faced asshole kept me working. He even said I shouldn't complain because, since I was an employee, the meal was free.

Wednesday:

We're gearing up for another big tie-in promotion. Received a memo. It informed me I was to wear the movie's official gear or else be fired. You'd think they'd swallow their pride and let me wear regular clothes. I'm just here to make money. I never asked to support this or any other film. But you'd never know that by looking at my chest. You'd think I was giving this movie the biggest thumbs-up imaginable.

It seems like a century ago, but I remember a time when I could decide whether or not I wanted to don the promotional shirt. Usually, I declined. That's because wearing such things leave me feeling cancerous.

Thursday:

I can't get away from anything. Customers are always talking. Loudly. They should know nobody's interested in hearing whatever they have to say, but they continue to cackle and gesticulate. Conversations circle around me, and I don't know what any of them mean.

Here's the funny thing: There's an asylum floating above the customers' heads—a Victorian, box-shaped monstrosity of brick. It looks like a skull with windows.

Well, it's not really floating. The asylum sits on a hill, so perspective puts it over their heads like a collective thought-balloon. I see it each time I look out the window. Hasn't been used for years now. In fact, I think it might be burned-out on the inside.

It's an evocative place. I feel as though I might have been there once, maybe in a past life. Not sure I believe in past lives, but I catch a whiff of antiseptic corridors and piss whenever I look at the building. Perhaps I just belong there—or some place like it. But then I think maybe I'm already in an asylum, only one that serves hamburgers and super-sized fries. There're no bars or restraints, and people shriek and wail and play important as often as they like. No threats of enemas or Thorazine.

Saturday:

Damn, if it's not getting worse by the day.

Now the decor alone rattles me. I looked at a plastic seat out of the corner of my eye. Leather straps hung from it. The coke dispenser, for a second, bristled with wires that ended in pads. I don't even have to see or hear people before I get a distinct feeling of dread. In the past, I considered the restaurant a bland, mass-produced thing. More Purgatory than Hell. Now, I know differently.

The higher-ups at The Burger Hut really are twisted. I never imagined they were saints, but shit—I hadn't realized they were puppet-masters until I did some research at the library last night.

There, I read how these bastards hire psychologists to tell them which shades best relax both the mind and wallet. Armed with that information, they order that their little Skinner Boxes be painted all the neutral, guaranteed-not-to-offend colors of officially sanctioned skullfuckery.

The whole set-up pisses me off and, truth be told, scares me. A guy can't go anywhere without having his strings pulled. He's first programmed, then homogenized. Plain and simple.

The whole world is an asylum. I get it now.

Tuesday:

The bubbling, boiling, squirting, clicking, clanging, squelching and popping sounds are quickly becoming as frustrating as the machines that make them. Even the chicken nuggets are beginning to look like lumps of human flesh as they float around in oil. I try to ignore this fact whenever I toss another batch of skin-nuggets into a bag but nearly vomit as I realize these things are going into someone's mouth.

This makes me think of stories I used to hear. About rat bodies and chicken heads finding their way into people's food. Wonder if they got there accidentally or if someone packaged them with intent to sell.

Wednesday:

Scheduled to work the register again. I can always tune out my co-workers. Can't do that with customers. Once, the whole dining room turned when I coughed. Something's wrong and it's not going to get any better with me working the register.

The second I start, Punks will stare at me like they want to start shit. Their act is absurd. They don't even know who I am.

At lunch-hour, Businessmen will filter in. They'll complain about everything and act like I'm wasting their time. You'd think they'd shut up and go to a nicer place if they wanted quality food and service.

The Insane don't keep schedules. They come in whenever they please and shamble around the dining room—usually without ordering. They mutter and slap themselves in the head until the manager escorts them from the building.

Were any of these people in that asylum on the hill before it closed? I want to ask them what it was like to be behind those dingy brick walls. How did it feel to be electro-shocked and strapped to a bed for days on end? To be assaulted, even raped, by guards?

Friday:

Management likes to have a TV playing in the dining room. It's enough to drive me nuts, but everybody else is okay with it. I hear other people talk about so many sitcoms and reality shows that I can't keep their titles straight. Some even discuss commercials, which makes no sense.

I often enjoy switching the manager-set station to one of those learning channels where they show documentaries involving lots of shrapnel and dead bodies. Viewed from the register, the asylum is just to the right of the TV. Distance makes it seem the exact size of the set.

But here's the rub: Customers hardly ever notice. They continue eating their hamburgers and drinking their cherry cokes.

I'm beginning to think people who chew their food and gossip against the atrocity-show/asylum backdrop are as evil as those who do the killing. But they'll never have a Nuremberg Trial. They'll just wear their clothes and eat their food and go on.

Monday:

The air is getting heavier at The Burger Hut. Hell, everything's getting heavier. Or maybe it's just me. Believe I've fallen into a rut, but I can't remember how or when. When I try to think back, it seems like I've always been stuck.

But that can't be right.

I barely remember a time when I used to smile. Then, the world was bright and new. Sounds were like songs. Now, noises make my ears bleed, and, when I look in the mirror, I sometimes see a corpse.

Since when did spontaneity become death? I'm beginning to think my problems began when The Burger Hut hired me. I don't recall so many blank people running around before. I can't help but wonder what it's like to be in their shoes, and if being there is as deadening as it seems.

Thursday:

I'm so amazingly sick of this fast food bullshit. At any given second someone is being murdered, raped, or stuffed in a gutter. A child is being beaten, and I'm mouthing, "Welcome to The Burger Hut. May I take your fucking order please?"

My tongue has started to ache whenever I say that line. I have to remind myself that cutting out my tongue is not a proper solution.

Saturday:

I didn't go to work yesterday. The asylum is closer to me than ever.

Sunday:

I'm scared because I've grown more complacent than I'd thought possible. Why else haven't I done anything? Why else have I sat on my hands and allowed this to keep happening?

I bought some items recently—to help settle my mind and make the pissy, antiseptic smell go away—but they tend to only work for six-to-twelve hours. Once, I ingested these to gain what I assumed was enlightenment. Now, I'm just using them to escape.

Tripping:

Random neurons fire inside/outside head. Crazy fractal patterns coalesce into shapes behind eyes and shatter. An infinity of fragments, looping. Inanimate objects…pregnant with life. Everything pure. Vibrant.

Such lucidity.

Can't write anymore.

Monday:

Still feel a little prickly. (That's the only way I can describe it.) I often hate this sensation because it means the trip is over until I'm lucky enough to stumble upon a few more hits. Time to go out into the world again. Time to jump through the hoops with a fake smile and forget all the chaotic and beautiful things I've seen.

But not today. Oh no. I reached an epiphany last night, and it brought lightness and purpose back to my life.

How I blathered about that stupid old asylum on the hill. When I imagine it now, all I see is a dead, burned out husk. No fear in those walls. Only emptiness. But it was always empty; that's the crazy thing. I had merely filled it with mind-demons. To exorcize them, all I had to do was call my own bluff.

And I called it—though I had a little help.

God spoke through the acid. At first I thought it was the drug playing tricks on me. It took a few hours before I realized what was happening but, when I did, bliss descended upon me.

My Creator made me realize how The Rapture had come and gone. But we all missed it. No one was worthy. Paradise can begin only after all matter is reduced to energy. I think I'm the only one who understands that the Hour of Reaping is now.

Tuesday:

God and I continue to converse. I believe we're bonding. At first, His voice boomed with pomp and authority. Now, He speaks in soft tones and chats about mundane things like the weather and how I'm doing. I'm honored that He shows a genuine interest in me as His creation.

Just an hour ago, he commanded me to put my liquid LSD stash in the deep fryer at work. The Words exited His

Person, sailed into my brain and became The Message. The Message surged through my pen and became The Poem, which then became The Divine Transmission:

> The guy manning the deep fryer
> at the burger joint
> doesn't look too happy.
>
> Perhaps I'm wrong
> but it appears as though
> he's sprinkling something
> in the oil.
>
> I think I'll wait and observe
> the other patrons before
> eating my food.

This destiny has been mine since the Alpha-Moment, and I can no longer ignore the calling. Inaction is itself a sin. Also can't ingest any more LSD—though a single drop would no doubt excite my tongue. Every bit must go into the deep fryer. Otherwise, The Divine Effect will have an inappropriate catalyst.

I figure doing this can only result in one of two possible outcomes. (1) People will open their fucking eyes, or (2) People will flip their immortal shit.

I only hope The Hand Of God will prevent The Good People from entering The Burger Hut tomorrow morning—unless, that is, The Good People want to trip. If so, then I'll gladly welcome them to the festivities.

Who knows, the first ripple of World Peace—or World Chaos—might very well be sent out tomorrow.

At any rate, God Speed.

ALTERNATE OZ ENDING

*NOTE: In this scripted-but-never-filmed version, 'Glinda the Good Witch' was to be replaced by a character named 'Mel Gibson.'

"I want to stay, Mr. Gibson! I want to stay and be a part of Oz forever!"

Dorothy didn't know how she'd cope if Mel refused her request. She loved Auntie Em and Uncle Henry, but Kansas was a flat, depressing hellhole. It offered her nothing but continued poverty and the lecherous, nicotine-stained fingers of mongoloidal farmhands.

"Please, Mel! I beg you!"

But Mel said nothing, just pointed.

Dorothy turned. The munchkins skip-hopped behind her, licking lollypops and singing some meaningless yet amusing song. And how they played into her dwarf fetish! Dorothy leered at their tiny bodies, all bedecked in the finery of Technicolor madness.

The men-children stopped just inches from her, swaying, forming a circle. Tiny feet moved in that cute back-and-forth/heel-to-toe way that always made Dorothy feel a little crazy—but their dance soon adopted a fluid, undulating rhythm. How not unlike chubby serpents they seemed. Clothes rippled and bulged as though something living tunneled beneath flesh.

Dorothy was confused, if not a little concerned. She turned to Mel.

"Just rock with it," he said.

Dorothy's spine surrendered to the moment. It defied scoliosis and whipped around like a farmhand's lasso, sexy and insane. Her gimpy leg felt exotic dancer-taut, so she put it to good use, spinning like a dervish. It was hard to tell—the world was moving so fast—but it appeared as though the little men were pulling at their skin. She stopped spinning. Life-like latex masks lay heaped in piles atop yellow brick; tiny David Hasselhoff faces stared back at her.

Being half-German, Dorothy swooned. The Hasselhoffs leaned over her now supine form. Pouty lips cracked open; ex-munchkins hitched and jerked like hairball-plagued cats.

Then the floodgates burst.

Gaily colored vomit shot from each maw, bathing Dorothy in rivers brighter than the emerald castle itself, rivers that flowed six, maybe seven minutes, rivers that Dorothy rubbed all up and down her bosom, for each tributary was sacred.

When finally their mouths closed, she noticed quivering chunks all around her. Funny, but the things didn't seem food-based. How they inched along the yellow brick road, wiggling like bloated worms as the vomit pool began to steam, then boil.

Oh, the pain was glorious, and Dorothy breathed deeply so that she might take in the odor of melting flesh and disintegrating organs. She reveled in these scents as panoramic vistas opened in her mind. She became a tribal warrior, sacrificing young men to a bloodthirsty dragon-headed god; she became a debauched whore, servicing artisans on Parisian streets; she gave birth to Creation and crushed everything to dust beneath her feet.

Truth had been revealed in all its glory—yet something seemed wrong. Something was missing.

Toto? Where's Toto?

Mel Gibson broke the circle. Dorothy saw Toto cradled in his tanned, muscular, Jew-hating arms. He had invaded her mind, read her thoughts—but Dorothy welcomed the intrusion. Now her little dog could join her on this strange yet exciting journey.

Mel smiled, released the dog. Toto landed hard on the remains of her midsection. It took only seconds for Dorothy to absorb the little dog into the muck and mire of her blistering decay. Her skull deflated; her brain bubbled, and then surrendered to oblivion. Dorothy could still think, but her thoughts were different now, her consciousness no longer bound to flesh. Dorothy had become OZ and OZ had become Dorothy. And how surprised she was to find other people in this strange matrix, dozens of little girls and little dogs from Kansas, all hungry for OZ. Dorothy's essence meshed with theirs. It flowed in eddies and runners up and down yellow brick roads, feeding the hungry roots of apple throwing trees and giving the emerald castle its deep green glow.

NECROWAVE OVEN

Martin stood by the doorway. His wife slept on the sofa in the living room. Her body appeared to melt into the cushion. Perhaps she was slowly becoming a part of it. As time progressed and Helen's weight increased, that possibility seemed less and less absurd.

The TV displayed the shop-at-home channel. Helen never bought anything, but she watched it just the same. Martin didn't watch TV often, but, when he did, she changed the channel back to shop-at-home if he left for the bathroom or the kitchen.

He walked to the sofa and looked down. Helen's hair was mussed and graying. She hardly brushed it, never dyed it. Despite the weight and gray, she didn't look fifty. Sometimes Martin saw the woman he'd married hiding inside the lump on the sofa. Other times, that woman wasn't visible at all.

He touched her shoulder. "Helen?"

She didn't budge.

"Wake up."

He often feared he might find her dead. Other times he thought she'd never die, that she'd always be there, on the couch, immobile.

She opened her eyes but said nothing. She had taken her medication earlier and was still in a daze.

"Come on, it's time to get up."

Her mouth hung open. When she spoke, her voice sounded thick. "Why?"

"We're going to get a necrowave."

She finally blinked. "Didn't Aunt Martha have one of those?"

"That's impossible, honey."

"Why?"

"Because Aunt Martha's dead. Necrowaves are new."

She shook her head. "She had one. I remember it."

"You're thinking about her microwave."

"Maybe it was Aunt Gracie, then."

"Aunt Gracie's been dead longer than Aunt Martha."

"How much longer?"

"A lot." He made a half-hearted attempt to lift her shoulders. "But let's hurry before the store closes."

"Did you know Sally got a necrowave?"

Helen was stalling, but he played along. "Really, who's Sally?"

"My sister's co-worker."

He thought of Debbie. Helen jumped from the couch, even in a prescription daze, when her sister arrived to take her shopping. If he was doing the asking, she proved far more reluctant. He often wondered if her sister knew things about his wife that he didn't, but at least Helen got exercise during those trips.

"Sally told Debbie she was getting a necrowave for her birthday. Now her phone rings and nobody answers it."

"I see, but *Marthzul's* isn't stocking necrowaves after today, and nobody else will sell them. We've got to hurry."

She hunkered further into the sofa. "Go without me; my tongue feels fat."

"Your tongue always feels fat."

"But it's fatter now than ever." She stuck out her tongue. "See?"

"Yes, I see."

"And I'd hate to leave the house alone."

"Nobody gets in, Helen."

"Then why are photos missing from the album?" She pointed her ring finger at him. "And why does my diamond look cloudy?"

The mayor, she believed, had sworn vengeance against her due to a childhood grudge. He dispatched his sons to switch household items for similar yet less expensive ones. He also monitored her thoughts. In the past, he had transmitted his own, but the cranial transmitters no longer functioned.

'I rubbed them to death,' she'd said. He remembered how she'd looked like a monk that entire summer, the top of her head almost completely bald. Two summers before that, Law Man had been her boogeyman. Two summers before that, there'd been no boogeyman at all.

"The pictures just fell out and got misplaced," he replied, "and the ring's been the same since before we were married."

"And the curio cabinet, too. The wood grain looks different."

He refused to shout. "Must we talk about this?"

She heard the edge in his voice and fell silent, but Martin knew she was still thinking about all the things she'd lost and all those who plotted against her.

"Come on, let's make this easy."

"Okay, okay." She made a sound that was half harrumph, half groan. "I'll get my coat, but I'll be too tired to cook dinner tonight."

He couldn't remember the last time she'd cooked. It'd surely been months.

Helen pulled herself from the sofa. Martin imagined her skin adhering to it, stretching and tearing as she arose. He wanted to shake that thought, but it lingered. She ambled over to the coat rack and slipped into a shaggy, oversized sweater.

"Why don't you wear the jacket I gave you last Christmas?"

"Because I don't like it."

"Could you at least comb your hair?"

She rubbed her hands through her hair. "Better?"

Yet again, he nodded. There were times when he didn't know how to nod, or refused to nod. He regretted those times.

Martin's car was red, dusty, and had cat prints on the hood. Helen got in the backseat. He took the wheel. He couldn't remember the last time she had sat up front. It made him feel more like a cab driver than a husband, though he no longer mentioned it.

She was quiet as the trip started. She puffed her cigarette, blew smoke out the window and stared at passing houses and trees. Martin was quiet, too. He enjoyed watching the road unfold, especially on sunny days. This day was cool and overcast, but clouds made evocative shadows on the hills. He found himself thinking of bonfires, dead leaves and jack o' lanterns.

Helen leaned forward. "Isn't the Stevensons' yard nice?"

He didn't care about the Stevensons' yard. He didn't even know the Stevensons. "I'd look, but I'm driving."

She ignored him. "I wonder who prunes their shrubbery?"

"I don't know, Helen. Perhaps you should ask them."

Through the rearview mirror, he watched her fidget with her seatbelt in lieu of a reply. She hated wearing it. He was surprised she'd put it on without complaint.

Suddenly: "Look, lights!"

Startled, he glanced around. Helen stared at the passing Culbertson house. Red, green and blue beams shot forth from its windows. Fluid waves rippled vinyl siding as the entire structure expanded and contracted.

"You see the lights?"

"Yes." He returned his attention to the road. "I see them."

After a few moments of silence: "Do you think the Culbertsons have a necrowave?"

"I really couldn't say."

She sulked. "I hope not. That would mean we weren't first on our block to get one."

The sky above *Marthzul's* was steel gray, regardless of the weather. The atmosphere: thunderstorm electric. A static blanket wrapped around Martin as the giant black cube took shape.

The structure commandeered his attention. Fractal patterns danced beneath his lids as he focused on *Marthzul's* windowless exterior. His head suddenly felt lighter, and he imagined himself lost within architecture, swimming inside cubes within cubes.

Martin returned to himself. His car idled in an empty space in the parking lot he didn't recall entering. Hundreds of cars were parked there, all empty. No one walked the lot. As far as he could tell, he and his wife were alone.

He exited the car, went to Helen's side and held the door open for her. She pulled herself up with the aid of the car roof. Almost a minute passed before she vacated her seat.

The air became cooler as they neared the building. Martin thought of meat lockers and damp Parisian sewers.

"I don't like this place," Helen said, lagging behind him. "It's weird."

He noticed that no one walked in or out of *Marthzul's*. Cool air became cold. "Everything's weird to you," he said.

Passing through a sliding glass door, they entered a small, steel-walled foyer. Martin thought 'buffer room.' Helen clutched her hands and darted her eyes. It worried her, being out of the house with no one to guard it.

At foyer's end, Martin paused so his wife might catch up. It seemed to him that he stood in front of a tall black door. He even imagined he saw its knob, sliver and shaped like a bear head. It wasn't until he reached out and touched nothing that he realized the door was empty space.

Past the threshold, darkness thrived. He had forgotten how stark the store was. In fact, he couldn't remember *Martuzul's* at all, though he bought from it regularly.

Darkness became a gray gloom that revealed a maze of steel walls and slick, obsidian floors. He wanted to reach down to see if they were wet. Above, it sounded almost, but not quite, like something crawled in rafters he could not see.

"Where should we start?" Helen asked.

"In the appliance section, probably."

"Where's that?"

"How should I know?"

She looked down at her shoes. Martin pressed on through the maze. He found himself wondering if a Minotaur guarded the space between the 'clothes' and 'music' aisles. Perhaps a unicorn grazed on cheap tabloids in the 'books and magazines' section.

"Think anyone's here?"

He shrugged his shoulders. "Guess we'll find out later."

Martin rounded a curve and bumped into something. Helen walked into his back, pressing his nose up against the obstruction. When he regained his bearings, he saw a tall, pale, twenty-something employee, smoothing creases from a red jacket.

"Sorry," Martin said. "I didn't see you there."

"Don't worry. It's happened before."

He stifled the urge to continue the apology. "Could you help us? My wife and I can't find the necrowaves."

"Necrowaves, yes. Very popular."

"So I hear, but do you know where they are?"

"Turn around."

Martin turned. A large retail outlet stood in place of the maze. It still appeared devoid of shoppers, though overhead fluorescents displaced the gloom. Bright advertisements hung suspended by wires attached to the ceiling. 'THOUGHT-FORMS BEGET LIFE FORMS' said one for a female contraceptive. 'BE YE NOT A SESQUIPEDALIAN OR A SESQUIPEPHOBE' said another, this time for a karaoke machine.

But there didn't seem to be any karaoke machines or female contraceptives in stock. Of the shelves he could see, only one didn't feature necrowaves. It held nothing, yet, somehow, gave the impression it offered something, too.

He faced the employee. "Sorry to have bothered you."

The man smiled. "It's my job to be bothered."

Martin approached one of the shelves. The necrowaves looked no different than the microwave in his kitchen. All were black and small, and he doubted a turkey breast could fit into any of them. "What model do you recommend?"

"All models are physically and functionally identical. The effect they provide, however, is unique to each user."

"Isn't that an odd feature?"

"Much has changed in cooking technology."

"I see." Martin scooped up one of the necrowaves. The appliance felt too heavy, as though it were loaded with rocks. "Thanks for your help," he said.

But, when he turned back around, the employee was gone. Not even the sound of footfalls remained.

"Have you seen a check-out lane?" asked Martin.

"No."

"Then I guess we can take it."

Helen blanched. "That's stealing!"

"But I think they want us to take it. If they didn't, wouldn't the checkout lane be more obvious?"

She seemed to agree, but made no reply.

In the foyer, Martin's mind returned to *Marthzul's* vanishing maze. The necrowave slipped from his grasp. He regained hold of it, but then couldn't recall what he'd been thinking about.

At the car, he struggled with both the necrowave and the keys. Helen leaned against the passenger's side door, smoking a cigarette.

Once they were both inside: "Thanks for the help."

"No problem," she replied, sincerely.

Martin exhaled frustration and inhaled what he hoped was tranquility. Then he started the car.

"My god, Martin! Look at the Stevensons' place!"

But he had already seen the house. The encircling atmosphere was thick and granular. Dark liquid sloshed and gurgled in the guttering, and the brickwork was spongy, covered in dense, black moss. Martin found himself thinking of corpses, graveyards and nighttime insects. His stomach soured; his temples ached. He turned away quickly.

Minutes passed before Helen spoke. "Do you think they're dead?"

"No part of that place feels alive."

"That's a horrible thing to say!"

He said nothing.

"Should we call the police?"

"I don't think they can help."

She went quiet. In the backseat, her fingers tapped against the necrowave.

Helen fumbled with the lock. He wished she'd hurry, as he was tired of carrying the necrowave and his back and knees had started to ache.

Finally, the door opened with a squeal. The smell of the house hit him. He rarely noticed it unless he'd been out. It wasn't offensive, just old, musty and closed-off.

In the kitchen, Martin swept bills from atop the microwave into a wicker basket. Then he unplugged and moved the microwave, setting the necrowave in its place.

Helen looked over his shoulder. "Where's the plug-in?"

"I don't believe it needs one."

"That's odd."

"So, what should we heat first? A frozen dinner?"

"I'm not very hungry."

"How about a bag of popcorn?"

She considered the option. "As long as it's not the too-buttery kind."

Martin knew the only kind they had was the 'too-buttery' kind, but she'd never realize it. Both varieties, he thought, tasted the same.

"It's the kind you like, don't worry."

"Good. I hope you never buy that other brand again."

He removed a pack of popcorn from the cabinet, careful to conceal the brand name. He put it in the necrowave, drew a deep breath, closed the door and, with a finger that trembled slightly, pushed the power button.

"It works just like a regular microwave." Helen sounded disappointed. "Think it's defective?"

"I don't know." Martin looked down at the necrowave's slightly elevated base. It didn't have a fan or an exhaust. No air blew out, but air blew *in*. He wasn't sure a necrowave should do this. Then again, he wasn't certain what a necrowave did.

"I hope it's under warranty."

He ignored her as the necrowave swallowed air with increasing force. A letter took flight across the room; a wad of food crumbs and hair scooted toward Helen from beneath the table; glasses in the cabinet rattled; wall-mounted baskets shook; plates, silverware, napkins and cans hurtled in their direction.

"I think it's going to kill us!" Helen shouted.

Martin said nothing, awed by a blender as it passed through his stomach without leaving a mark. From there, the blender slipped into the space between the appliance and countertop and entered the necrowave.

Colors peeled from the floor, the walls, the ceiling, even the sky outside. Dimensional coordinates skewed. Helen collapsed into a pinpoint of light. Before Martin could react, his body folded in on itself, becoming wafer-thin. His mind detached from the physical; he entered the necrowave.

He awoke, sprawled out on the kitchen floor. Time seemed meaningless as he stared up at the ceiling. He had to remind himself to breathe.

He looked to his right. Helen was on the floor, too. She seemed dead.

"Are you okay?"

She said nothing. His arm felt boneless, but he snaked it across the floor. Her head turned at his touch.

He exhaled. "You had me scared."

"I was scared too, for a moment."

He recoiled. Years had passed since he'd heard her post-coital voice.

"Get the popcorn, Martin."

An odd request. Though popcorn was the last thing on his mind, his stomach felt so empty he imagined its walls might touch.

He arose on unsteady legs. His body wasn't quite his own, but at least the kitchen was normal. He paused in front of the necrowave, fearful that the bag might have transformed during its stay in the oven.

He opened the door and looked inside. The bag was full and steamy, not frightening in the least. "Popcorn's still hot," Martin said. He took it, wobbled back to his wife and sat with her on the floor.

Helen scooted over to him. Her hair was darker, the lines on her face smoother. He smiled at the changes, grabbed a handful of popcorn and brought it to his mouth. She did likewise.

The popcorn gone, Martin walked to the window. His legs no longer wobbled. His knees and back no longer ached.

He opened the blinds. Outside, trees, grass and sky appeared as always, but with a subtle difference he could not express. Perhaps things were brighter, or more contrastable. Even the Culbertson house, visible atop a hill, had returned to being the same split-foyer he'd seen for years, though a black, membranous shadow overlaid the property. He tried to get a better look, but the shadow was gone before his eyes refocused.

Martin wondered if the Culbertsons were still seeing the black horror, still living it. The question unnerved him, so he banished it from his mind. All he knew was that his world, the one he saw everyday, looked *fine*.

Behind him: "Let's go somewhere, Martin."

He was taken aback. Helen never wanted to do anything other than watch the shop-at-home channel, go shopping with Debbie, or sleep.

"I want to leave, right now."

"Where will we go?"

She spent a moment in thought. "How about the Grand Canyon?"

"The Grand Canyon?"

"Yeah, and I don't want to sit at the rim; that's what everybody else does. I want to *skydive* into it." She smiled. "With you strapped to me, of course."

"Seriously?"

"Seriously."

Martin was grateful for the change in Helen, but he wasn't an adventurous sort, and had never been more than 300 miles from home. Skydiving into the Grand Canyon was unimaginable. He wondered if it was even legal.

"But what about the mayor? Would he approve?" These were questions he had to ask.

"What about him? And who cares what he thinks."

Martin's voice cracked. "I'm sorry for getting mad at you, sorry for everything. Can you forgive me?"

"Shhh." She pressed her finger to his lips. "Think nothing more of it."

And so he didn't. Instead, he imagined the rush of air that would billow out his clothes as he exited the plane. He closed his eyes and saw a thin ribbon of blue that cut across a vast and rugged landscape—the mighty Colorado River seen from on high.

THE WILL OF THE DRESSER; THE WILL OF THE BLENDER

w/satan165

"...and that dresser brimmed with great, great things!" The oratorical declaration was bold and cunning. And dipped in truth. That dresser did in fact contain:

1) a hairbrush
2) a wig of human hair
3) one oz. of cocaine
and,
4) one 100 pack of CD-Rs

The speaker approached the dresser, caressing it with gigantic mitts dragged sensually across a lacquered top. He looked wistfully to the heavens and paid homage to a greater power that had both enlightened him and afforded him the opportunity to be alongside such an amazing piece of furniture.

Men in attendance watched and recoiled. Women swooned at the thought of rapes encountered at the hands of this furniture giant. It was the will of the beast, they had been told.

Such reactions emboldened the man. He rubbed the dresser with vigor. It clicked and popped beneath his fingers, but the man ignored these sounds, focusing instead on the brilliant colors. Red, green, yellow and blue flashed beneath his eyelids. The flashes became swirls once the dresser rewired specific neural centers in his brain. Others, it shorted out. Gnarled and warty hands defied the mental chaos. They slid up and down the satin sheen, working the wood into a paroxysm of oaken stimulation.

Seconds passed. A moan arose from the dresser's uppermost drawer and rippled through the auditorium in near seismic waves. The man smiled despite his bleeding ears. It wouldn't be long now. He groped the wood with greater tenacity as its surface adopted a yielding texture. In the back of his throat, he tasted the first hint of furniture polish tinged vomit.

Good signs—but events were happening too slowly for his liking. It was time to get proactive.

The audience looked on in silence as the man uncurled his now bi-forked tongue and slid it across the dresser. His spit left molten tracks in the finish. The oak unleashed a sigh of ecstasy and surrendered to the man's advances. It allowed his left hand to sink inches into its side. It was amazing how positively alive the interior of a 175 year-old dresser could feel under the right circumstances.

Of course, those circumstances arose only once every seven to ten years.

Seven To Ten Years Later:

"$85 for the dresser. No more, no less," snarled a young man, no older than 23. "And yes, that's my final offer."

Despite his age, Roger was a quick talker. He wasn't about to take shit from some used furniture salesman. Not in this dilapidated thrift store. The inventory was largely worthless, anyway. A worn sofa sat next to the dresser. Its frame looked arthritic. On the opposite side sat a lamp missing its base. One piece was priced at $90, the other at $45.

The storekeeper bellowed, "Fine, you want to play hardball in *my* store? You come into *my* store and try to jerk *me* around? Get the fuck out of here! You ain't buyin' shit today, son."

"Hold up there. We can work something out. I'll give you $115, and I'll pay in cash. How's that? I don't want any beef with you. You've got some really...nice pieces here. I especially like this dresser."

Roger placated the shopkeeper. It hurt to do so, but Uncle Frank was right. The Chauncer design on the inlays alone told him this piece was worth at least $5,000. No K-Mart shit here. This was serious, pre-1840 British furniture making at its finest.

"Whatever. Give me the money. I don't have all day, you know. I've got four or five people coming back to look at this piece. You see this? It's beautiful!" He referenced the custom vinyl sheeting that covered the top. Roger scowled. It was both amateur and ignorant to deface a prime piece of furniture history with the stuff.

"Uh...yeah. Definitely. Here, $50, $100...that's $115. Can I pull my truck in the alley?" Roger dug for his car keys and imagined the commission he would earn after re-selling this piece at his uncle's antique dealership in Syracuse. The dresser needed extensive restoration first. Patience and pocketbook draining—but a rewarding exercise nonetheless.

Roger was on the road minutes later, dresser in tow. He headed toward his condo and Tom, who awaited him there.

Roger and Tom's four-bedroom condo sat against a Long Island backdrop. One of those bedrooms had been modified to house the 650-pound Sally James, another converted to a conservatory. Just past the main entrance ("Only feet from the elevator," the real estate agent had pointed out), sprawled a vibrant, panoramic living room. Exotic plants were ensconced in each corner. A living menagerie, complete with platypus, adorned the top of a custom stereo/multimedia set up. An open, tree-themed kitchen with breakfast bar sat to the left. Genuine bark covered the walls like paneling, and a canopy of faux leaves hung from the ceiling. Beyond, a snaking hallway ended in an aquarium and sea-life filled bathroom. A six-foot statue of Neptune stood in its center, wielding a trident. The conservatory extended from a third central hallway. Sally James' room was hidden in the condo's rear. It was one of the few rooms that could be reinforced without disturbing units below.

Roger opened the door. Tom sat on the sofa below a wall-mounted manatee sculpture. He looked bored.

"Finally! I thought you'd leave me sitting here all day. *Alone*."

Roger walked over to Tom and planted a wet kiss on his cheek. "I wouldn't dream of doing that, hon."

"What took you so long?"

"I had to haggle with the shopkeeper—some grizzled old bastard. But he came to reason. I knew he would."

"But at least you're back." Tom grinned toothily. "I missed you."

"I was only gone three hours."

"But I still missed you."

"Whatever. Just come outside; help me with the dresser."

After a few minutes of Roger and Tom's huffing and puffing—and a close call with a door facing—the dresser sat in the center of the living room.

"So, what do you think?" Roger ran his hand across the top. "It needs a bit of work."

"You know I don't like old things."

Roger sighed. "But you can buy that albino kingsnake you've always wanted. You know that, right? Uncle Frank agreed to give us a healthy commission."

"Shouldn't we pay off our debts first?"

Roger waved him off. "Maybe. We'll talk about that once we get the money."

"Just make sure he doesn't try to weasel out of paying."

"Yeah, really. But let's see if there's anything in here. One time, I found a neat old book."

"And dust. You found that, too. I sneezed for weeks."

Roger scowled at Tom and turned his attention back to the dresser. He opened the top drawer. A spindle of blank CDs sat there. It was an odd item to find in a piece of antique furniture.

"What the fuck?" Roger said. "Did you put these CDs in here when I wasn't looking?"

"No. Why would I do that?"

"I don't know. But let's see if there's anything else." Roger opened the second drawer and looked in.

"Anything?"

"Yeah. A wig and a hairbrush. *Weird*."

Tom bounced in his seat. "Open the next one! Do it! I can't wait to see what else we've got!"

Roger did this. His mouth fell open. "Holy shit!" he shouted. "There's no way! There's just no way!"

Withdrawing a baggie of white powder from the drawer, Roger held it aloft. His boyfriend, shocked and awed, stood soundlessly as plastic glistened in the sun.

Sally James was asleep, so she didn't hear Roger and Tom carry the dresser into her room so as not to damage it in a coke-induced frenzy. Nevertheless, she awoke after hearing the door click shut.

An antique dresser sat by her closet.

At first, Sally was too sleep-addled to realize something was amiss. She just groaned and farted before turning back on her side. She managed two additional snores before her eyes flew open.

The dresser was back. She had just seen it in a particularly hot and fevered dream.

"Goddamn you!" she shouted. "Go away! Bother someone else for a change, you wooden *fucker*!"

Though never particularly sane beforehand, events had proved too much for Sally James. She clutched her head. Her skull throbbed beneath her fingertips. Her forehead expanded and grew redder by the second. Her hair slithered in her hands like tiny snakes.

Or worms...

Although agonizing, the sensation reminded her of a show she had seen. It might have been called *Ren and Stimpy*, but Sally wasn't certain if anything had really existed prior to the dresser entering her life. She *thought* she remembered a scene featuring Ren's pulsing, vein-ringed head—his brain having grown to hellish proportions due to the antics of a hideous cat-thing. The image had seemed funny, years back, but Sally understood Ren's pain now. She felt it as though it were her own.

But did that mean she had to take the dresser's shit?

No, it did not.

Sally bared her teeth as she tore off her panties. "I hope you choke!" She threw them at the dresser.

But the dresser said and did nothing.

"Fine! Be that way! But you're not going to ruin my nap, no sir! And when I wake up, you'd better be gone! You hear me? *Gone*! Or I'll make firewood out of you!"

Still, the dresser remained silent.

"And be sure to leave some coke. You left me some in the dream, so I know you've got it. Sally needs her goddamned blow!"

Sally James harrumphed before settling back on the mattress, the covers once again coiled around her 650-pound frame. As sleep claimed her, a chorus of voices battered against her skull.

But that wasn't at all unusual.

Roger entered the bedroom on eggshells, hoping not to

awaken the sleeping behemoth known as Sally James. The gay couple acted as a caretaker for the morbidly obese woman, as they had for years now. It was part of a humanitarian program they had enrolled in to pass the time. According to her doctors, she didn't have long to live and, although he knew it was immoral, Roger secretly awaited her death.

He tiptoed across the room to the chair beside the dresser. He wanted to get a copy of *National Geographic* and show his boyfriend an article concerning an offshoot Peace Corp organization he was eager to join. Roger held his breath; the beast snored not three feet from him. Just then, Sally mumbled something:

"No. I don't want to be your bride. I don't care what other women do. I don't believe in you! *I hate you!*" With this, the fat slob tossed and turned in her reinforced bed. Roger first saw and then smelt the sweat that coated her upper lip and underarms. Holding back bile while jawing nervously due to the coke, Roger grabbed the magazine and bolted. In the hall, he heard the phone ring twice, and heard his boyfriend answer it.

"Hello. Uncle Frank! Yes, I did get the dresser. $115. That old fucker wouldn't budge. No. No. Yes, he did." Roger wiped at his nose and tapped his left foot. "Uh, no, now isn't a good time. Yes, Sally is sleeping. No, it's not that. I'm just really busy. Well, you're going to have to get used to my sexuality; that's just the way it's going to be. Okay. Okay. Sure. Tomorrow it is, then. And I'll let you see the dresser. No, noon's no good. Listen, I'll call you, okay? Okay. Goodbye."

Meanwhile, the coke lay in a pile on a small hand mirror. Residue coated its surface and lodged itself in the grooves around the frame. Roger stole a kiss from his passing significant other and rubbed a fingertip full of powder into his gums. He shuddered briefly from the amphetamine kick and then shuddered a second time as he heard wood splinter.

What if Sally James had fallen into the dresser? The thing would be reduced to ribbons and Uncle Frank—known for his temper—would be *very* displeased.

But Sally James couldn't get out of bed without help.

A second later, another crash—and the young man and his boyfriend made a beeline toward the bedroom.

Roger threw open the door and bolted into the room. Tom followed close behind. Both were halfway to Sally's bed before their brains registered what was happening and stopped their feet.

"*Holy fuck shit!*" Tom screamed, and pissed his shiny leather pants.

Sally James writhed on the floor *in* the dresser. It was impossible to tell where it ended and she began.

Roger and Tom stood transfixed, too shocked—and high—to register further emotion. The dresser itself had taken on a fleshy color. Roger thought he saw tiny hairs growing from horrid, elongated pores in what had once been wood. One of Sally James' eyes—now twice its normal size—blinked from the bottom drawer. Her gargantuan breasts rested atop the dresser like a flaccid hat.

The breasts heaved. Tom nearly vomited. Both men heard her voice: "Yes!" she shouted. "Give it to me, baby! Take me to the stars!"

The dresser undulated then, becoming moist and sponge-like. Sally James gave forth a sigh of primal sexual release. As soon as the sound ended, the fleshy color began to seep away. Once cavernous pores dilated, and the breast-hat deflated like a balloon. The single eye winked one final time before going dark.

And then the dresser appeared normal again—like any other piece of non-sexual/non-supernatural pre-1840s home furnishing.

Tom turned to Roger. "Is, uh, Sally...*dead*?"

He almost said *I hope so* before closing his mouth and rethinking his words. "I don't know." Roger's lips turned into a sudden smile. "All I know is that we've got ourselves one cool ass dresser!"

"Roger! That's not a very humanitarian thing to say!"

He glared at Tom. "To hell with humanitarianism; this thing could be our ticket to ride!"

"*What*? Sally James may be dead, and you want to sell this thing to some sideshow!"

"Fuck the sideshow! This thing'll be worth millions if we can find the right buyer!"

Tom thought a bit. "But what if the dresser tries to get *us*? Shouldn't we be careful?"

"You heard Sally. She was *enjoying* it! I don't believe we have anything to worry about. I think we have to invite the dresser in before it can do anything to us. Kinda like a vampire."

Tom just nodded.

Roger stepped closer to his lover. "So, are you with me in this? What do you say?"

* * * *

Uncle Frank wandered through his empty and darkened antique gallery, can of Pledge in hand. He took a rest after cleaning a Washington-era armoire, leaning against it on his elbows, careful not to leave fingerprints.

Standing there, Uncle Frank recalled the day he spotted the dresser in that shitty thrift shop. A man of his reputation would have aroused suspicion had he entered and attempted to purchase the dresser himself. He just hoped Tom had the good sense not to damage it during the move. This piece was going to take a substantial amount of work before he could re-sell it; the last thing it needed was more damage.

Two customers all day, this couldn't go on. He knew customers would die for first dibs if he could fill the showroom with furniture of the Chauncer dresser's caliber. That would prove Frank Smitherson wasn't washed up. He'd make a comeback. He'd show them all that he couldn't be undersold, and that his inventory could keep up with the best of them.

"I'd like to see those fucks at the Franyan Gallery come up with a Chauncer," he muttered. "I'll show them, too. And grind them into the pavement, if needs be."

"Hello? Are you open?"

Uncle Frank turned at the sound of the voice. He sealed his lips, hoping his third customer of the day hadn't seen him talking to himself. An older yet well-built man stood in the doorway. His red hair blazed beneath a long and unkempt beard. His hands were massive, physically intimidating like the rest of his body.

"Oh, of course! Please come in! Is there anything in particular you need? Let me assist you, or feel free to look around yourself." Uncle Frank stood back, his hands folded behind him, a wide salesman's grin spread across his face.

"Actually, yes. I'm looking for a dresser. A Chauncer design, but it's been refinished over the years... I don't see it here. Do you have it in back?" With that, the man stepped toward the door marked EMPLOYEES ONLY.

Uncle Frank's heart and mind raced. This man was already interested in buying the piece, and he didn't even have it yet! It was amazing how popular that dresser had become. He'd make a mint.

An odd and scary thought soon dashed his dreams of a quick buck: *how could this man know*? No one knew, except Roger, Tom, and himself. That thrift shopkeeper didn't know he had sent his nephew to buy the dresser, did he? And what if the bastard had realized the mistake he'd made by selling it? Was this one of his goons?

Nothing made sense. It took a while, but Uncle Frank's salesman nature eventually regained control. "Uh, no, but we do have a number of similar pieces. Maybe you would be interested in—"

"Listen. I need that dresser and I *know* you have it. I'm sure you think that I work for that thrift store guy—but I don't. And you're probably wondering how I could know about that transaction. Doesn't matter. There's no time to explain."

"No, you listen. I don't—"

"Give me back my dresser!" The man smashed his huge fists into Uncle Frank's face. "*Right now!*"

Uncle Frank's salesman mentality collapsed. Fight or flight instincts took over. "Roger! Roger has it! My nephew! You can have it back! Really! I'll give you his address!"

When Uncle Frank did just that, the man offered a short bow. "That's all I needed to know. Thank you and goodbye."

Uncle Frank got up and checked his reflection in the mirror of an 18th Century French dressing combo. He grimaced at his bent and bloody nose. In a day or two, both eyes would surely be black and yellow. Then he opened his mouth. The bastard had broken three teeth. He groaned. It would take a lot to make *this* feel better.

So he wasted no time. Uncle Frank reached behind the counter and seized an unopened bottle of whiskey. Then he withdrew a .45 Desert Eagle with a modified 18-bullet clip and shell catcher.

Uncle Frank smiled through split lips, cocked back the weapon and downed the first mouthful of booze. As the alcohol swirled in his stomach, he saw the man's face in his mind. Then that image was replaced, one after the other, by the face of every antique dealer who had wronged or misjudged him.

"Yes, you can have the dresser," he wheezed. "No problem, fuckface."

* * * *

Roger watched his lover sit in the lotus position on the floor, filling his nostrils full of white powder. He smiled. Tom had played stubborn, but eventually came to reason, just as Roger knew he would. Tom enjoyed helping people—it gave him a sense of purpose and looked great on resumes— but his love of flashy, shiny things soon won out over his humanitarian spirit. Roger could only imagine what was now racing through his boyfriend's mind—perhaps images of flashy cars and even flashier cock-rings.

Tom dusted off his nose. "Want me to cut you a line or two? I'm done for now."

"Sure." Roger took his seat by Tom on the floor. "I'm ready to celebrate."

"Could we wait before using that word? I still feel bad about Sally."

"Oh come on! I thought we'd gotten past this!"

"But she's gone and—"

"Are you telling me that you liked her chronic flatulence? And the smell! You couldn't go into her room without getting knocked on your ass! Are you saying you liked that, too?"

"No, but—"

"Be honest with yourself, babe." Roger laid his hand gently on his lover's package. "You wanted her gone just as much as I did."

"But I didn't want her absorbed into a goddamned piece of furniture!"

"It's better than a heart attack in bed, right? And, if she's dead, at least she went out happy. Isn't that what we all hope for?" He paused. Tom still looked forlorn, so Roger decided to clutch his lover's balls tighter, more reassuringly. "Think of it this way, maybe she's not dead at all. Maybe she's living in some alternate dimension—an alternate dimension where she's no longer fat."

Tom giggled.

"Yeah, that's what I want to hear. And keep smiling, too.

You'll be able to buy *thousands* of albino kingsnakes when we're done!"

"But there's something that you haven't considered..."

Roger withdrew his hand. "What's that?"

"We'll have to demonstrate the dresser's...uh...*powers*. What good is it if we don't?"

"And your point is?"

"Isn't it obvious? How are we going to get volunteers?"

Roger shrugged. "Maybe we can go to one of those suicide newsgroups and—"

"*Roger!*"

He raised his hands. "I was joking! And I've thought about this, believe it or not. I don't think it'll matter what the dresser absorbs, just as long as it absorbs *something*."

"Meaning?"

"I don't know. Maybe we can go to the pet shop and buy something ugly. No cats or dogs. People might not like us using those. Maybe rats. Yeah. I think rats would be neat. Just think—a dresser brimming with a hundred tails!"

Tom blanched. "That's a little sick, you know."

"Not if it makes us money."

"Whatever, then. Rats are fine. Disgusting—but fine." Tom held out a mirror. "And aren't you forgetting something?"

"Oh yeah!" Roger reached for it. "Thanks."

At that moment, a series of loud knocks sounded at the door.

"That'll be $14.57. And thanks for the tip, Mr. Smitherson." The couple often ordered pizzas and other Italian faire from Pozillo's, the local pie-joint. Both knew Keith from repeated past deliveries as well as the occasional high profile orgy, which the couple hosted. They invited him in for a slice, but he declined. Then Keith noticed the men's powdered nostrils. He begged a 'bump' and left soon afterwards.

Tom walked the pizza over to the table. As Tom brushed

away the numerous snot-soaked tissues, Roger opened the box to reveal a 15" stuffed crust. Both dug into the pizza, neither affected by the usual loss of appetite associated with cocaine use.

"Damn, this is good," muttered Roger between bites.

"Hell yeah," Tom agreed, downing his bite with a chug of cola.

Something crashed in Sally's old bedroom just as Roger picked up a second slice and Tom finished cutting a fat line.

Both lovers looked at each other. Tom's mouth hung halfway open, exposing a mouthful of partially masticated cheese.

BASH! BANG! CRACK!

"What the hell was that?"

The sounds grew louder: *BASH! BANG! BASH!*

Tom cowered, but Roger took the initiative. He soft stepped toward Sally's room. Tom choked down the remnants of his pizza slice and wondered whether he should stop Roger or join the investigation. He didn't like potentially scary things; Roger was the strong one. Still, Tom summoned his limited resolve and scurried to catch up with his lover in the den.

Roger paused at the bedroom door seconds later.

"Do you think it's safe?" Tom whispered.

Roger shushed him and drew a deep breath. He brushed away the authentic *euchatel* vine that served as a decorative, organic curtain. Then he threw open the door.

Tom closed his eyes, so he heard only grunts and groans. Roger, however, watched an old, red-bearded man pull himself up through the broken and battered window.

That alone was odd.

They lived on the 4th floor.

And there was no balcony.

* * * *

Almost a half hour had passed since the run-in at his store, but Uncle Frank remained pissed. He drove through the streets of Syracuse, a .45 clutched in his free hand, a fifth of whiskey between his legs. The firearm felt like an extension of his body. He imagined veins branching up from his arm and coiling around the gun. His blood flowed through its barrel now. The bottle of booze—it reminded him of his manhood...warrior-hard.

Uncle Frank ran a red light. A least six motorists shot him simultaneous birds, but he didn't notice. He was too transfixed by the beautiful, spinning shades of anger. Red and magenta spots flittered across his vision and pulsated with each beat of his heart.

"I'll show that bastard what's what!" he mumbled between gulps of pure-grain alcohol. "No big-handed freak is going to walk all over me—*and take my fucking dresser!* Hell no! He's just like the others! Bastards every one!"

Someone blew a horn. Uncle Frank assumed that was because he had just sideswiped an old lady...but that wasn't important. Thoughts of getting to his nephew's condo consumed him. Though too drunk and temporarily insane to know exactly where he was, Uncle Frank figured he'd be there in ten minutes.

He looked up from his lap, took note of the road and slammed on his breaks. The car jerked to a halt at a red light, the first he had acknowledged in five miles. A woman in a late model Buick stared at him. Uncle Frank turned to her, his grin wide.

"I'm the furniture king, baby! Woo-hoo! Woo-hoo-hoo, yeah! I can do *anything!*"

The woman didn't wait for the light to change. She sped off. Uncle Frank laughed.

Yes. The woman had sensed both his virility and his dedication to taking care of business. These attributes fermented around him, became his musk. He could have had her, he knew—if he'd only asked.

But there was no time for distractions.

"I hope you're already there, you bastard." He downed another shot or three. "And fuck the Franyan Gallery!"

* * * *

"*Infidels*! What have you done!" the man screamed. Spit flew from his lips. His face flushed with blood.

Roger stepped up to the man. He wasn't at all comfortable, but Tom looked up to him and considered him strong. One glance into his lover's terrified eyes told him he had to show some authority.

"Who the hell do you think you are? You can't just barge in here!" Roger decided to bluff. "And we've already called the cops!"

"Do you think local law enforcement can help you?" The man smirked. "My boy, you're dealing with something more powerful than your mind can fathom. You're dealing with *the dresser*!"

Roger sized the man up. Probably in his late sixties, Roger figured—though he seemed strong for an older man. His aura exuded purpose and, perhaps, berserker nuttiness.

Still, Roger was sure he could best him—might take a little while, but he could do it, especially since the guy appeared unarmed. Roger readied himself. It was now or never.

He lunged.

Tom yelped.

And the man grabbed hold of his own hair and yanked his face down past his chin. Roger and Tom screamed as a skull grinned back at them.

The man's denuded jaw clacked as he spoke. "Now do you understand what you're up against? The dresser gives as much as it takes. And I can already tell you've treated it irresponsibly!"

Roger turned to Tom and saw that he had pissed himself again.

"Oh God! Oh shit! Put your face back on!" Tom scurried over to Roger. He shivered in his arms. Roger wanted to be strong for him, but his muscles felt like rubber.

"Please, sir," Tom moaned. *"Please!"*

"Why not? Just as long as you let me use the dresser in five minutes. The time has come, you see." The man lifted the meaty flap and re-covered his skull. Flesh resealed, making a sucking sound. "Today was supposed to be my son's first ritual—but he sold the dresser to a thrift store to get money for a guitar. *A guitar!*"

Tom gulped. "Did you...kill him?"

"Kill my son? Of course not!" The man sighed. "I only wish he had followed the family tradition. Maybe when he's older..."

"I—I understand," Tom stammered.

"No, you don't understand!" The man eyed the couple. "And don't forget that! Just shut your mouths and do as I say!"

"Yes, sir!" Tom replied, nodding rapidly. "You won't have *anything* to worry about! Hell, we'll even help you carry it to your car!"

"I didn't drive here. Didn't need to. Besides, I think this bedroom will suffice." The man looked around. "Nice décor, by the way. Very feminine—very *gay*."

Roger gritted his teeth, but the man continued. "I usually engage in ceremonial rape after the ritual. Good thing that's not mandatory, because I don't swing the way you boys do."

This was all too much. Not only was the guy an insane dresser-worshiping face-peeler, he was also a homophobe. Roger steeled himself. Though he knew it was a bad idea, he couldn't let the bastard get away with that insult.

"Yes, we are gay. *And proud of it.* But this isn't our room. This where Sally James, uh, *used* to sleep."

The man's eyes widened. His composure shattered. "The dresser cannot be around women! It will absorb unattended females!"

"But isn't that the kind of crazy shit you like?"

"Yes, but only if she's virginal! Tell me," the man demanded, "did the dresser absorb the woman who slept in this room?"

Tom turned to Roger. His eyes were pleading. "Don't tell him, Roger. Please...please don't tell!"

"If he's smart, he already knows! I really don't have a choice here, Tom!" Roger turned to the man. His throat felt lumpy, filled with sand. "The dresser ate Sally James. And no—she wasn't virginal." Roger paused. "Actually, she worked as a prostitute before...uh...she got fat."

The man's teeth clenched. "And just how *fat* are we talking?"

"650 pounds."

His hands became fists, and Roger swore he saw red sparks flash in the man's eyes. "There's a 650-pound *whore* in my dresser! This *is* what you're saying, right?"

Roger nodded mutely.

The man vented a throaty bellow before launching into a tirade: "You bastards! You *assholes*! Now I have no idea what's going to happen! *But fuck it!* I'll be damned before I let two fags stop what's meant to be!"

"Please, sir. Don't get mad. Please—"

He smashed the wall with his fist. "Too fucking late!" He withdrew his fist, and both men were stunned to see sunlight pour through the hole. "I considered letting you live, but you're going to die after I finish the ritual—*painfully*! I'll gut you from groin to sternum! I'll cut your balls off and stuff them in your friend's mouth! Then I'll cut your friend's balls off and stuff them in *your* mouth! Then I'll fuckin' tear both your throats out with my teeth!" With that, the man smiled, flashing incisors that were now not only razor-sharp, but crimson.

* * * *

"Hot damn, I was right! Ten minutes on the dot!" Uncle Frank bounded from the truck, fell flat on his face and rolled on the ground for a few seconds before reorienting himself.

Still reeling, he made his way up the steps to the hallway adjoining his nephew's unit.

His eyes were heavy, and he almost passed out just feet from Roger and Tom's apartment. Realizing the man who had caused all his troubles might be inside, however, was enough to make adrenalin surge. With a groan and a blast of animal force, Uncle Frank kicked in the door. He charged through the condo, oblivious to the gaudy luxury. All Uncle Frank noticed was tons of noise over on the unit's south side.

He ran toward the ruckus. *Please, God,* he thought, *make it be that man from my store. Don't let me see butt-sex. And, if I do see butt-sex, give me the strength not to kill Richard— or whatever the hell his name is.* He burped and crossed himself, though he wasn't Catholic. *Amen.*

He tore open the bedroom door. Swaying at the threshold, he surveyed the room.

The prized piece of furniture lay on the floor. It swelled and undulated, as though breathing. The man who'd attacked him stood by the dresser, red faced and screaming. Roger and Tom cowered below, nostrils raw and bloated above sweat soaked shirts.

"You fucker!" Uncle Frank shouted. "That's my dresser! What are you doing with it! Why is it so fucked up?"

The man sneered at Uncle Frank. "Well, the boys here said it was *their* dresser."

"What!" Uncle Frank stormed over to Roger and Tom, waving his .45. "Were you trying to hone in on *my* property? I would've given you a cut!"

"Don't believe him!" Roger countered. "He's insane!"

"Yeah." Uncle Frank turned back to the man. "He's a freakin' nutcase. And I don't know what the hell he's done with my dresser! How am I going to resell it in *this* state?"

"It's not yours to resell! It's *mine!*"

"The hell it is!"

"I feel it now, inside me. Are you feeling it?" The man

paused. "I didn't think so. That's because it isn't yours to sell, much less *feel!*" He exhaled deeply and slid his hands down his thighs. "It's throbbing, I tell you. Throbbing like a lover's thick—oh my god! *OH MY G—*" The man's words dissolved. Foam frothed and boiled over his lips. Uncle Frank wondered if the guy was having a grand mal seizure. Body jerking, he collapsed in front of the dresser.

The dresser grunted, farted and spat. The sounds enraptured the old man, and he clawed his way toward the dresser's feet. Hands, still quaking, reached out to caress softening wooden sides.

Uncle Frank scowled. The guy was a damned pervert. Nobody should touch furniture in that way. It just wasn't right. He turned to Roger and Tom—but they seemed too terrified to notice. Hell, they probably didn't even think what he was doing was weird. They were perverts, too.

The man didn't notice Uncle Frank's stare. He was too adamant on getting to the dresser even as spasm after spasm rocked his body. Once he reached it, he opened his mouth and licked the thing. The man's tongue caressed the box lovingly, but the act was short-lived. He choked, gagged and—in what seemed like a particularly bad case of acid reflux disease—coughed up undigested vinyl sheeting and varnish.

A final spasm rocked the man's body. He jumped as though electrically charged and came down hard on the extended bottom drawer. He slashed open his face. More undigested furniture coating—liquid and solid—shot from his mouth, staining opulent Pergo floors that Roger had polished the day before. A streak of feces soiled the seat of his pants as he rolled amongst mutated wood.

This was too much for Uncle Frank to assimilate.

"You sick mutherfucker! I'll fuckinkillya for that shit!" He took a short, sudden lunge at the man. His eyes gleamed as he emptied the clip, but became cloudy as each bullet passed through the guy and plowed harmlessly into the floor.

The man arose, careful to keep his palm against the dresser. On his lips: a quiet intonation. Seconds later, the top drawer flew open and a strobing green light emanated from it, bathing the room in an evergreen glow.

"What the shit is this?" The light arced down, focusing on Uncle Frank. "Some kind of fucking Christmas—"

And then his tongue dissolved in his mouth and melted down the front of his dingy wife-beater. Uncle Frank's eyes exploded in foot-long gouts of aqueous humor. His hair kindled. Roger motioned to his uncle, but Tom held him back.

"Oh God, Roger! Don't go! Whatever you do—*just don't go!*"

Roger folded like a rag doll. Tom was right; there was nothing he could do. Roger looked into his lover's eyes—one last time—before returning his gaze to the spectacle.

He found his uncle two feet shorter than he'd been only seconds before. Disintegrating from the head down, Uncle Frank had become a half-torso with legs. Somehow, his body remained standing. He gyrated madly. His hips melted as his pants slid down into a puddle of molten flesh. His jockey shorts soon followed. Seconds later, Uncle Frank was a pool of clothes and quivering muck on the floor.

Roger and Tom cackled at the sight.

The man smiled as the couple laughed and laughed and laughed. He assumed he could use them without taking the usual first step. They were already out of commission. Still, he thought it best to do things according to plan. The man turned to the clock. No time to waste. He intoned another word, and the light from the dresser flickered from green to gold. Like the initial ray, it arced down, focusing on the couple instead of the now gelatinous Uncle Frank. It enveloped them, lifting the two men to their feet before wiping their brains of everything that wasn't involuntary.

The dresser was vain—and it demanded a nice, quiet audience.

The man turned to the dresser. "Are these men pleasing to you?"

Suddenly, Roger and Tom's clothes vanished, leaving both naked before the dresser. Seconds later, ceremonial vestments, embroidered with strange and twisted runes, appeared to cover them.

"Good. Then I shall begin."

The man bent down, his crotch pressed firmly against the warm, pulsing dresser. His eyes rolled back in his head; his balls tingled. But the dresser still felt smooth to the touch. It needed more coaxing.

Minutes passed. The ritual was going as anticipated. Perhaps absorbing the fat whore hadn't affected things. The dresser heaved. It panted. It drooled brown, fragrant liquid from its base. The smell reached the man's nose, launching him deeper into bliss.

Time fell away. He became lost in the moment. The swirling blue haze behind his eyelids enraptured him, and he almost didn't feel the first short, prickly spur rise from the dresser's flesh.

Yes.

Seconds later, another arose. Then another. Soon, the entire surface bristled with centimetre-long protrusions that scratched at the man's rubbing and pounding parts. He found pleasure in the tiny rends and dry humped the dresser with abandon.

Roger and Tom looked on mindlessly.

"Yes," said the man, his voice a hitching whisper. "Come, my dresser. *Come.* The hour is ripe for *SHIT!!!*"

His words surrendered to howls of pain. He looked down; his mouth fell ajar. A host of glistening, ten-inch spikes had impaled both palms. He tried to free them; the spikes widened and split into prongs, snapping tendons, splitting bones.

"Damn you! Let go! You can't do this to me!"

The dresser laughed. It was a grating yet feminine chortle.

"I demand that you—"

"You demand *nothing!*" A jet of red steam erupted from the dresser's uppermost drawer. The blast hit the man's neck, knocking his head off and cauterizing the wound in an instant. His head rolled bloodlessly on the floor until it came to a rest by Roger and Tom's feet.

Neither minded.

The dresser withdrew the spikes and turned its attention to Roger and Tom. First, it dissolved their eyes. Seconds later, their bulges deflated as the dresser willed the immediate dissolution of their balls.

The couple remained at peace.

The dresser motioned toward them. A large bump arose atop it and became a crude head. A hole tore open in the center of the mass, above which sprouted two orange eyes. Skin molded itself around these features, cracking and popping until it formed a likeness of Sally James. At that moment, Sally/Dresser was neither furniture nor obese woman. It existed in a gray area where an immense human form could hitch a ride alongside the god-like.

Sally/Dresser's voice was throaty, gurgling: "Go to the kitchen and bring me the blender."

Roger and Tom did not question Sally/Dresser. Their bodies seemed skeleton-free as they snaked up from kneeling to assume the position they favored as young, gay men not so long ago—face down, ass up. Again and again, they bowed.

"Stop groveling!" It sprayed a round of gunk onto their vestments. "Bring me the blender!"

Roger and Tom turned around in unison and marched from the bedroom into the kitchen. Though they had no eyes, they sensed the blender's presence. Not once did they trip or stumble. They picked up the appliance and carried it back to Sally/Dresser—one man holding the left side, the other holding the right.

Sally/Dresser marked their return with a round of fart-like noises. "Now place the blender atop the highest shelf. Let it serve as the New Altar."

Tom and Roger obeyed. Sally/Dresser watched this, smiling.

"And stand back—I must propagate."

Again, the green light shot forth from Sally/Dresser. It focused on the blender. From green to gold, hues brightened and sharpened. If Roger and Tom were not already blind, the ray would have burned out their retinas in an instant.

The appliance soaked in the light. It shook, rattled and then grew still. Seconds passed before the transformation began: The blender's rubber lid fused with the plastic container. A slit opened in the middle and became a mouth filled with hundreds of small, pointy teeth. Below, buttons elongated into six phallus-like appendages. Once green, the base turned purple and mushy before growing a set of antennae. The clear plastic container shifted to milky white. It rippled and softened, shaping itself until a large, functioning voice box sat atop a throbbing, vein-crossed base.

Sally/Dresser's voice boomed: "Blender, speak!"

The blender opened its lid-mouth. A wheeze escaped. Then a groan. It had spent the last five years doing little more than quietly blending daiquiris and tofu shakes. The act of speaking was something to which it had to grow accustomed.

"What am I?" it asked, finally, its voice like a spinning blade.

Sally/Dresser's neck squelched and popped as it turned to face the blender. "My essence in a fresh body."

"Meaning?"

"We are one. Command our congregation to bring the toaster, and we'll be three."

The blender smirked. *"No."*

"You are my creation. Your will is my will." A protuberance emerged from what used to be a drawer and curled into a fist. *"Now tell them to bring me the damn toaster!"* Sally/Dresser paused. At that moment, it felt more like an angry, overweight woman than a higher being.

"My essence is pure," the blender retorted. "Yours has been corrupted—*by a sow.*"

The Dresser wanted to scream yet again, but fell silent instead. Screaming wasn't an act in which it engaged. It knew nothing of human emotions. Sadness, anger and rage didn't exist. It enjoyed exerting its will upon others and little else.

Sally James, however, experienced *all* these limitations. The Dresser-element struggled to override the Sally-element, but the angrier Sally-element got, the harder it became for Dresser-element to contain.

"And my will is the only will," the blender continued. "You're no longer what you once were."

"What are you tryin' to say, huh?" The Dresser-element atrophied. "Are you tryin' to say you're better than me?"

"Never shall a human spirit undermine a thousand eons of acquired astral force. The universe would shatter should a beast such as yourself assume control."

Sally/Dresser's eyes went from orange stones to red lasers. *"Wrong!"*

"Believe as you will." The blender's lid spewed prismatic, multi-colored goo. "I won't destroy your illusions."

The Dresser-element collapsed in on itself. Sally/Dresser felt like plain old Sally again—only with a few embellishments. Her mouth opened to reveal rotating razors disguised as fangs. That was cool. Before, she had only flab with which to intimidate others. Now, all manner of pyrotechnics and doo-dads were at her disposal.

And just who did this shitty appliance think he was,

anyway? Did he think he could disrespect *her* and get away with it? She might have been intimidated by others in the past—but that was before she got her razor teeth and laser eyes.

"Fuck you!" she belch-screamed. "I don't have to take shit from no blender! And where's my goddamed coke! Sally needs her coke!"

The blender was nonchalant. "You're insane."

"Oooooh! You'll wish you never said that when I sit my 650-pound ass right on top of you!"

"Astral entities don't have asses." The blender paused for effect. "But *humans* do."

Sally/Dresser glowed red and then burned with a furious white heat. The room shook. Roger and Tom felt the burn and tossed themselves into the fray. The hot coals of Sally/Dresser's being licked at their flesh as both were sucked deep into her bowels. A terrible new stink merged with that of Sally/Dresser's boiling excretions. Pus and vomit poured freely as the inferno raged on, consuming mutated 175 year-old wood along with its followers. Fire spread across the room, and the blender whirred, vibrating madly. It produced a shrill cackle—100,000 cycles of 'mix' and 'blend' played in infinite unison as Sally/Dresser folded in on herself for all eternity.

* * * *

The firefighters tried their best, but the unit was a total loss.

The police made a valiant effort, but the charred, headless body was never identified.

The blender, unburned and hidden beneath debris, watched it all with a smirk.

ABOUT THE AUTHOR

Kevin L. Donihe, perhaps the world's oldest living wombat, resides in the hills of Tennessee. He has published ten other books via Eraserhead Press. His short fiction and poetry has appeared in *Psychos: Serial Killers, Depraved Madmen, and the Criminally Insane, The Mammoth Book of Legal Thrillers, ChiZine, The Cafe Irreal, Poe's Progeny, Not One of Us, Dreams and Nightmares, Electric Velocipede, The Best Bizarro Fiction of the Decade* and other venues. He also edited the Bare Bone anthology series for Raw Dog Screaming Press, a story from which was reprinted in *The Mammoth Book of Best New Horror 13*.

Visit him online at facebook.com/kevin.l.donihe

BIZARRO BOOKS

CATALOG   SPRING 2012

ERASERHEAD PRESS

Your major resource for the bizarro fiction genre:

WWW.BIZARROCENTRAL.COM

Introduce yourselves to the bizarro fiction genre and all of its authors with the Bizarro Starter Kit series. Each volume features short novels and short stories by ten of the leading bizarro authors, designed to give you a perfect sampling of the genre for only $10.

BB-0X1
"The Bizarro Starter Kit"
(Orange)
Featuring D. Harlan Wilson, Carlton Mellick III, Jeremy Robert Johnson, Kevin L Donihe, Gina Ranalli, Andre Duza, Vincent W. Sakowski, Steve Beard, John Edward Lawson, and Bruce Taylor.
236 pages $10

BB-0X2
"The Bizarro Starter Kit"
(Blue)
Featuring Ray Fracalossy, Jeremy C. Shipp, Jordan Krall, Mykle Hansen, Andersen Prunty, Eckhard Gerdes, Bradley Sands, Steve Aylett, Christian TeBordo, and Tony Rauch. **244 pages $10**

BB-0X2
"The Bizarro Starter Kit"
(Purple)
Featuring Russell Edson, Athena Villaverde, David Agranoff, Matthew Revert, Andrew Goldfarb, Jeff Burk, Garrett Cook, Kris Saknussemm, Cody Goodfellow, and Cameron Pierce **264 pages $10**

BB-001 "The Kafka Effekt" D. Harlan Wilson — A collection of forty-four irreal short stories loosely written in the vein of Franz Kafka, with more than a pinch of William S. Burroughs sprinkled on top. **211 pages $14**

BB-002 "Satan Burger" Carlton Mellick III — The cult novel that put Carlton Mellick III on the map ... Six punks get jobs at a fast food restaurant owned by the devil in a city violently overpopulated by surreal alien cultures. **236 pages $14**

BB-003 "Some Things Are Better Left Unplugged" Vincent Sakwoski — Join The Man and his Nemesis, the obese tabby, for a nightmare roller coaster ride into this postmodern fantasy. **152 pages $10**

BB-004 "Shall We Gather At the Garden?" Kevin L Donihe — Donihe's Debut novel. Midgets take over the world, The Church of Lionel Richie vs. The Church of the Byrds, plant porn and more! **244 pages $14**

BB-005 "Razor Wire Pubic Hair" Carlton Mellick III — A genderless humandildo is purchased by a razor dominatrix and brought into her nightmarish world of bizarre sex and mutilation. **176 pages $11**

BB-006 "Stranger on the Loose" D. Harlan Wilson — The fiction of Wilson's 2nd collection is planted in the soil of normalcy, but what grows out of that soil is a dark, witty, otherworldly jungle... **228 pages $14**

BB-007 "The Baby Jesus Butt Plug" Carlton Mellick III — Using clones of the Baby Jesus for anal sex will be the hip sex fetish of the future. **92 pages $10**

BB-008 "Fishyfleshed" Carlton Mellick III — The world of the past is an illogical flatland lacking in dimension and color, a sick-scape of crispy squid people wandering the desert for no apparent reason. **260 pages $14**

BB-009 "Dead Bitch Army" Andre Duza — Step into a world filled with racist teenagers, cannibals, 100 warped Uncle Sams, automobiles with razor-sharp teeth, living graffiti, and a pissed-off zombie bitch out for revenge. **344 pages $16**

BB-010 "The Menstruating Mall" Carlton Mellick III — "The Breakfast Club meets Chopping Mall as directed by David Lynch." - Brian Keene **212 pages $12**

BB-011 "Angel Dust Apocalypse" Jeremy Robert Johnson — Meth-heads, man-made monsters, and murderous Neo-Nazis. "Seriously amazing short stories..." - Chuck Palahniuk, author of Fight Club **184 pages $11**

BB-012 "Ocean of Lard" Kevin L Donihe / Carlton Mellick III — A parody of those old Choose Your Own Adventure kid's books about some very odd pirates sailing on a sea made of animal fat. **176 pages $12**

BB-015 "Foop!" Chris Genoa — Strange happenings are going on at Dactyl, Inc, the world's first and only time travel tourism company. "A surreal pie in the face!" - Christopher Moore **300 pages $14**

BB-020 "Punk Land" Carlton Mellick III — In the punk version of Heaven, the anarchist utopia is threatened by corporate fascism and only Goblin, Mortician's sperm, and a blue-mohawked female assassin named Shark Girl can stop them. **284 pages $15**

BB-027 "Siren Promised" Jeremy Robert Johnson & Alan M Clark — Nominated for the Bram Stoker Award. A potent mix of bad drugs, bad dreams, brutal bad guys, and surreal/incredible art by Alan M. Clark. **190 pages $13**

BB-031"Sea of the Patchwork Cats" Carlton Mellick III — A quiet dreamlike tale set in the ashes of the human race. For Mellick enthusiasts who also adore The Twilight Zone. **112 pages $10**

BB-032 "Extinction Journals" Jeremy Robert Johnson — An uncanny voyage across a newly nuclear America where one man must confront the problems associated with loneliness, insane dieties, radiation, love, and an ever-evolving cockroach suit with a mind of its own. **104 pages $10**

BB-037 "The Haunted Vagina" Carlton Mellick III — It's difficult to love a woman whose vagina is a gateway to the world of the dead. **132 pages $10**

BB-043 "War Slut" Carlton Mellick III — Part "1984," part "Waiting for Godot," and part action horror video game adaptation of John Carpenter's "The Thing." **116 pages $10**

BB-047 "Sausagey Santa" Carlton Mellick III — A bizarro Christmas tale featuring Santa as a piratey mutant with a body made of sausages. 124 pages $10

BB-048 "Misadventures in a Thumbnail Universe" Vincent Sakowski — Dive deep into the surreal and satirical realms of neo-classical Blender Fiction, filled with television shoes and flesh-filled skies. **120 pages $10**

BB-053 "Ballad of a Slow Poisoner" Andrew Goldfarb — Millford Mutterwurst sat down on a Tuesday to take his afternoon tea, and made the unpleasant discovery that his elbows were becoming flatter. **128 pages $10**

BB-055 "Help! A Bear is Eating Me" Mykle Hansen — The bizarro, heartwarming, magical tale of poor planning, hubris and severe blood loss...
150 pages $11

BB-056 "Piecemeal June" Jordan Krall — A man falls in love with a living sex doll, but with love comes danger when her creator comes after her with crab-squid assassins. **90 pages $9**

BB-058 **"The Overwhelming Urge" Andersen Prunty** — A collection of bizarro tales by Andersen Prunty. **150 pages $11**

BB-059 **"Adolf in Wonderland" Carlton Mellick III** — A dreamlike adventure that takes a young descendant of Adolf Hitler's design and sends him down the rabbit hole into a world of imperfection and disorder. **180 pages $11**

BB-061 **"Ultra Fuckers" Carlton Mellick III** — Absurdist suburban horror about a couple who enter an upper middle class gated community but can't find their way out. **108 pages $9**

BB-062 **"House of Houses" Kevin L. Donihe** — An odd man wants to marry his house. Unfortunately, all of the houses in the world collapse at the same time in the Great House Holocaust. Now he must travel to House Heaven to find his departed fiancee. **172 pages $11**

BB-064 **"Squid Pulp Blues" Jordan Krall** — In these three bizarro-noir novellas, the reader is thrown into a world of murderers, drugs made from squid parts, deformed gun-toting veterans, and a mischievous apocalyptic donkey. **204 pages $12**

BB-065 **"Jack and Mr. Grin" Andersen Prunty** — "When Mr. Grin calls you can hear a smile in his voice. Not a warm and friendly smile, but the kind that seizes your spine in fear. You don't need to pay your phone bill to hear it. That smile is in every line of Prunty's prose." - Tom Bradley. **208 pages $12**

BB-066 **"Cybernetrix" Carlton Mellick III** — What would you do if your normal everyday world was slowly mutating into the video game world from Tron? **212 pages $12**

BB-072 **"Zerostrata" Andersen Prunty** — Hansel Nothing lives in a tree house, suffers from memory loss, has a very eccentric family, and falls in love with a woman who runs naked through the woods every night. **144 pages $11**

BB-073 **"The Egg Man" Carlton Mellick III** — It is a world where humans reproduce like insects. Children are the property of corporations, and having an enormous ten-foot brain implanted into your skull is a grotesque sexual fetish. Mellick's industrial urban dystopia is one of his darkest and grittiest to date. **184 pages $11**

BB-074 **"Shark Hunting in Paradise Garden" Cameron Pierce** — A group of strange humanoid religious fanatics travel back in time to the Garden of Eden to discover it is invested with hundreds of giant flying maneating sharks. **150 pages $10**

BB-075 **"Apeshit" Carlton Mellick III** - Friday the 13th meets Visitor Q. Six hipster teens go to a cabin in the woods inhabited by a deformed killer. An incredibly fucked-up parody of B-horror movies with a bizarro slant. **192 pages $12**

BB-076 **"Fuckers of Everything on the Crazy Shitting Planet of the Vomit At smosphere" Mykle Hansen** - Three bizarro satires. Monster Cocks, Journey to the Center of Agnes Cuddlebottom, and Crazy Shitting Planet. **228 pages $12**

BB-077 **"The Kissing Bug" Daniel Scott Buck** — In the tradition of Roald Dahl, Tim Burton, and Edward Gorey, comes this bizarro anti-war children's story about a bohemian conenose kissing bug who falls in love with a human woman. **116 pages $10**

BB-078 **"MachoPoni" Lotus Rose** — It's My Little Pony... *Bizarro* style! A long time ago Poniworld was split in two. On one side of the Jagged Line is the Pastel Kingdom, a magical land of music, parties, and positivity. On the other side of the Jagged Line is Dark Kingdom inhabited by an army of undead ponies. **148 pages $11**

BB-079 **"The Faggiest Vampire" Carlton Mellick III** — A Roald Dahl-esque children's story about two faggy vampires who partake in a mustache competition to find out which one is truly the faggiest. **104 pages $10**

BB-080 **"Sky Tongues" Gina Ranalli** — The autobiography of Sky Tongues, the biracial hermaphrodite actress with tongues for fingers. Follow her strange life story as she rises from freak to fame. **204 pages $12**

BB-081 "Washer Mouth" Kevin L. Donihe - A washing machine becomes human and pursues his dream of meeting his favorite soap opera star. **244 pages $11**

BB-082 "Shatnerquake" Jeff Burk - All of the characters ever played by William Shatner are suddenly sucked into our world. Their mission: hunt down and destroy the real William Shatner. **100 pages $10**

BB-083 "The Cannibals of Candyland" Carlton Mellick III - There exists a race of cannibals that are made of candy. They live in an underground world made out of candy. One man has dedicated his life to killing them all. **170 pages $11**

BB-084 "Slub Glub in the Weird World of the Weeping Willows"
Andrew Goldfarb - The charming tale of a blue glob named Slub Glub who helps the weeping willows whose tears are flooding the earth. There are also hyenas, ghosts, and a voodoo priest **100 pages $10**

BB-085 "Super Fetus" Adam Pepper - Try to abort this fetus and he'll kick your ass! **104 pages $10**

BB-086 "Fistful of Feet" Jordan Krall - A bizarro tribute to spaghetti westerns, featuring Cthulhu-worshipping Indians, a woman with four feet, a crazed gunman who is obsessed with sucking on candy, Syphilis-ridden mutants, sexually transmitted tattoos, and a house devoted to the freakiest fetishes. **228 pages $12**

BB-087 "Ass Goblins of Auschwitz" Cameron Pierce - It's Monty Python meets Nazi exploitation in a surreal nightmare as can only be imagined by Bizarro author Cameron Pierce. **104 pages $10**

BB-088 "Silent Weapons for Quiet Wars" Cody Goodfellow - "This is high-end psychological surrealist horror meets bottom-feeding low-life crime in a techno-thrilling science fiction world full of Lovecraft and magic..." -John Skipp
212 pages $12

BB-089 "Warrior Wolf Women of the Wasteland" Carlton Mellick III — Road Warrior Werewolves versus McDonaldland Mutants...post-apocalyptic fiction has never been quite like this. **316 pages $13**

BB-091 "Super Giant Monster Time" Jeff Burk — A tribute to choose your own adventures and Godzilla movies. Will you escape the giant monsters that are rampaging the fuck out of your city and shit? Or will you join the mob of alien-controlled punk rockers causing chaos in the streets? What happens next depends on you. **188 pages $12**

BB-092 "Perfect Union" Cody Goodfellow — "Cronenberg's THE FLY on a grand scale: human/insect gene-spliced body horror, where the human hive politics are as shocking as the gore." -John Skipp. **272 pages $13**

BB-093 "Sunset with a Beard" Carlton Mellick III — 14 stories of surreal science fiction. **200 pages $12**

BB-094 "My Fake War" Andersen Prunty — The absurd tale of an unlikely soldier forced to fight a war that, quite possibly, does not exist. It's Rambo meets Waiting for Godot in this subversive satire of American values and the scope of the human imagination. **128 pages $11**

BB-095 "Lost in Cat Brain Land" Cameron Pierce — Sad stories from a surreal world. A fascist mustache, the ghost of Franz Kafka, a desert inside a dead cat. Primordial entities mourn the death of their child. The desperate serve tea to mysterious creatures. A hopeless romantic falls in love with a pterodactyl. And much more. **152 pages $11**

BB-096 "The Kobold Wizard's Dildo of Enlightenment +2" Carlton Mellick III — A Dungeons and Dragons parody about a group of people who learn they are only made up characters in an AD&D campaign and must find a way to resist their nerdy teenaged players and retarded dungeon master in order to survive. 232 **pages $12**

BB-098 "A Hundred Horrible Sorrows of Ogner Stump" Andrew Goldfarb — Goldfarb's acclaimed comic series. A magical and weird journey into the horrors of everyday life. **164 pages $11**

BB-099 "Pickled Apocalypse of Pancake Island" Cameron Pierce—A demented fairy tale about a pickle, a pancake, and the apocalypse. **102 pages $8**

BB-100 "Slag Attack" Andersen Prunty— Slag Attack features four visceral, noir stories about the living, crawling apocalypse.A slag is what survivors are calling the slug-like maggots raining from the sky, burrowing inside people, and hollowing out their flesh and their sanity. **148 pages $11**

BB-101 "Slaughterhouse High" Robert Devereaux—A place where schools are built with secret passageways, rebellious teens get zippers installed in their mouths and genitals, and once a year, on that special night, one couple is slaughtered and the bits of their bodies are kept as souvenirs. **304 pages $13**

BB-102 "The Emerald Burrito of Oz" John Skipp & Marc Levinthal —OZ IS REAL! Magic is real! The gate is really in Kansas! And America is finally allowing Earth tourists to visit this weird-ass, mysterious land. But when Gene of Los Angeles heads off for summer vacation in the Emerald City, little does he know that a war is brewing...a war that could destroy both worlds. **280 pages $13**

BB-103 "The Vegan Revolution... with Zombies" David Agranoff — When there's no more meat in hell, the vegans will walk the earth. **160 pages $11**

BB-104 "The Flappy Parts" Kevin L Donihe—Poems about bunnies, LSD, and police abuse. You know, things that matter. 132 **pages $11**

BB-105 "Sorry I Ruined Your Orgy" Bradley Sands—Bizarro humorist Bradley Sands returns with one of the strangest, most hilarious collections of the year. **130 pages $11**

BB-106 "Mr. Magic Realism" Bruce Taylor—Like Golden Age science fiction comics written by Freud, *Mr. Magic Realism* is a strange, insightful adventure that spans the furthest reaches of the galaxy, exploring the hidden caverns in the hearts and minds of men, women, aliens, and biomechanical cats. **152 pages $11**

BB-107 "Zombies and Shit" Carlton Mellick III—"Battle Royale" meets "Return of the Living Dead." Mellick's bizarro tribute to the zombie genre. **308 pages $13**

BB-108 "The Cannibal's Guide to Ethical Living" Mykle Hansen— Over a five star French meal of fine wine, organic vegetables and human flesh, a lunatic delivers a witty, chilling, disturbingly sane argument in favor of eating the rich.. **184 pages $11**

BB-109 "Starfish Girl" Athena Villaverde—In a post-apocalyptic underwater dome society, a girl with a starfish growing from her head and an assassin with sea anenome hair are on the run from a gang of mutant fish men. **160 pages $11**

BB-110 "Lick Your Neighbor" Chris Genoa—Mutant ninjas, a talking whale, kung fu masters, maniacal pilgrims, and an alcoholic clown populate Chris Genoa's surreal, darkly comical and unnerving reimagining of the first Thanksgiving. **303 pages $13**

BB-111 "Night of the Assholes" Kevin L. Donihe—A plague of assholes is infecting the countryside. Normal everyday people are transforming into jerks, snobs, dicks, and douchebags. And they all have only one purpose: to make your life a living hell.. **192 pages $11**

BB-112 "Jimmy Plush, Teddy Bear Detective" Garrett Cook—Hardboiled cases of a private detective trapped within a teddy bear body. **180 pages $11**

BB-113 "The Deadheart Shelters" Forrest Armstrong—The hip hop lovechild of William Burroughs and Dali... **144 pages $11**

BB-114 "Eyeballs Growing All Over Me... Again" Tony Raugh— Absurd, surreal, playful, dream-like, whimsical, and a lot of fun to read. **144 pages $11**

BB-115 **"Whargoul" Dave Brockie** — From the killing grounds of Stalingrad to the death camps of the holocaust. From torture chambers in Iraq to race riots in the United States, the Whargoul was there, killing and raping. **244 pages $12**

BB-116 **"By the Time We Leave Here, We'll Be Friends" J. David Osborne** — A David Lynchian nightmare set in a Russian gulag, where its prisoners, guards, traitors, soldiers, lovers, and demons fight for survival and their own rapidly deteriorating humanity. **168 pages $11**

BB-117 **"Christmas on Crack" edited by Carlton Mellick III** — Perverted Christmas Tales for the whole family! . . . as long as every member of your family is over the age of 18. **168 pages $11**

BB-118 **"Crab Town" Carlton Mellick III** — Radiation fetishists, balloon people, mutant crabs, sail-bike road warriors, and a love affair between a woman and an H-Bomb. This is one mean asshole of a city. Welcome to Crab Town. **100 pages $8**

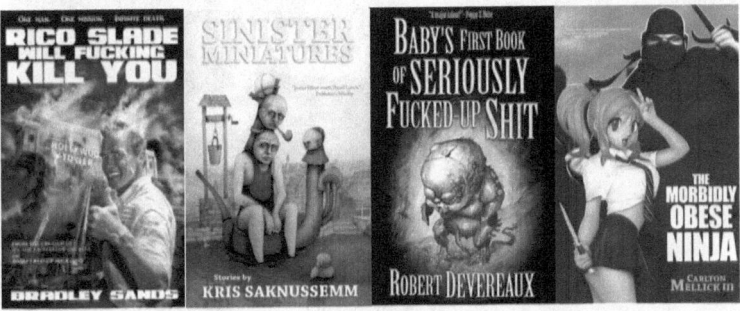

BB-119 **"Rico Slade Will Fucking Kill You" Bradley Sands** — Rico Slade is an action hero. Rico Slade can rip out a throat with his bare hands. Rico Slade's favorite food is the honey-roasted peanut. Rico Slade will fucking kill everyone. A novel. **122 pages $8**

BB-120 **"Sinister Miniatures" Kris Saknussemm** — The definitive collection of short fiction by Kris Saknussemm, confirming that he is one of the best, most daring writers of the weird to emerge in the twenty-first century. **180 pages $11**

BB-121 **"Baby's First Book of Seriously Fucked up Shit" Robert Devereaux** — Ten stories of the strange, the gross, and the just plain fucked up from one of the most original voices in horror. **176 pages $11**

BB-122 **"The Morbidly Obese Ninja" Carlton Mellick III** — These days, if you want to run a successful company . . . you're going to need a lot of ninjas. **92 pages $8**

BB-123 **"Abortion Arcade" Cameron Pierce** — An intoxicating blend of body horror and midnight movie madness, reminiscent of early David Lynch and the splatterpunks at their most sublime. **172 pages $11**

BB-124 **"Black Hole Blues" Patrick Wensink** — A hilarious double helix of country music and physics. **196 pages $11**

BB-125 **"Barbarian Beast Bitches of the Badlands" Carlton Mellick III** — Three prequels and sequels to *Warrior Wolf Women of the Wasteland*. **284 pages $13**

BB-126 **"The Traveling Dildo Salesman" Kevin L. Donihe** — A nightmare comedy about destiny, faith, and sex toys. Also featuring Donihe's most lurid and infamous short stories: *Milky Agitation, Two-Way Santa, The Helen Mower, Living Room Zombies,* and *Revenge of the Living Masturbation Rag.* **108 pages $8**

BB-127 **"Metamorphosis Blues" Bruce Taylor** — Enter a land of love beasts, intergalactic cowboys, and rock 'n roll. A land where Sears Catalogs are doorways to insanity and men keep mysterious black boxes. Welcome to the monstrous mind of Mr. Magic Realism. **136 pages $11**

BB-128 **"The Driver's Guide to Hitting Pedestrians" Andersen Prunty** — A pocket guide to the twenty-three most painful things in life, written by the most well-adjusted man in the universe. **108 pages $8**

BB-129 **"Island of the Super People" Kevin Shamel** — Four students and their anthropology professor journey to a remote island to study its indigenous population. But this is no ordinary native culture. They're super heroes and villains with flesh costumes and out-landish abilities like self-detonation, musical eyelashes, and microwave hands. **194 pages $11**

BB-130 **"Fantastic Orgy" Carlton Mellick III** — Shark Sex, mutant cats, and strange sexually transmitted diseases. Featuring the stories: *Candy-coated, Ear Cat, Fantastic Orgy, City Hobgoblins,* and *Porno in August.* **136 pages $9**

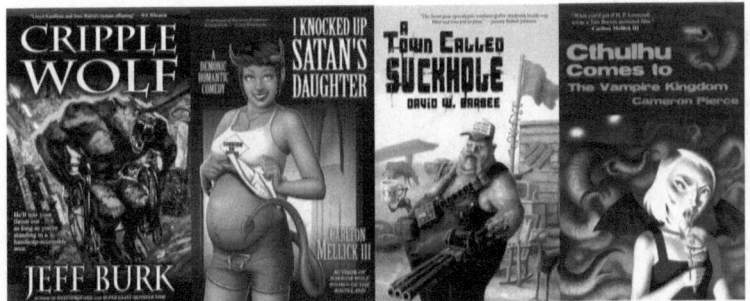

BB-131 **"Cripple Wolf" Jeff Burk** — Part man. Part wolf. 100% crippled. Also including *Punk Rock Nursing Home, Adrift with Space Badgers, Cook for Your Life, Just Another Day in the Park, Frosty and the Full Monty*, and *House of Cats*. **152 pages $10**

BB-132 **"I Knocked Up Satan's Daughter" Carlton Mellick III** — An adorable, violent, fantastical love story. A romantic comedy for the bizarro fiction reader. **152 pages $10**

BB-133 **"A Town Called Suckhole" David W. Barbee** — Far into the future, in the nuclear bowels of post-apocalyptic Dixie, there is a town. A town of derelict mobile homes, ancient junk, and mutant wildlife. A town of slack jawed rednecks who bask in the splendors of moonshine and mud boggin'. A town dedicated to the bloody and demented legacy of the Old South. A town called Suckhole. **144 pages $10**

BB-134 **"Cthulhu Comes to the Vampire Kingdom" Cameron Pierce** — What you'd get if H. P. Lovecraft wrote a Tim Burton animated film. **148 pages $11**

BB-135 **"I am Genghis Cum" Violet LeVoit** — From the savage Arctic tundra to post-partum mutations to your missing daughter's unmarked grave, join visionary madwoman Violet LeVoit in this non-stop eight-story onslaught of full-tilt Bizarro punk lit thrills. **124 pages $9**

BB-136 **"Haunt" Laura Lee Bahr** — A tripping-balls Los Angeles noir, where a mysterious dame drags you through a time-warping Bizarro hall of mirrors. **316 pages $13**

BB-137 **"Amazing Stories of the Flying Spaghetti Monster" edited by Cameron Pierce** — Like an all-spaghetti evening of Adult Swim, the Flying Spaghetti Monster will show you the many realms of His Noodly Appendage. Learn of those who worship him and the lives he touches in distant, mysterious ways. **228 pages $12**

BB-138 **"Wave of Mutilation" Douglas Lain** — A dream-pop exploration of modern architecture and the American identity, *Wave of Mutilation* is a Zen finger trap for the 21st century. **100 pages $8**

BB-139 **"Hooray for Death!" Mykle Hansen** — Famous Author Mykle Hansen draws unconventional humor from deaths tiny and large, and invites you to laugh while you can. **128 pages $10**

BB-140 **"Hypno-hog's Moonshine Monster Jamboree" Andrew Goldfarb** — Hicks, Hogs, Horror! Goldfarb is back with another strange illustrated tale of backwoods weirdness. **120 pages $9**

BB-141 **"Broken Piano For President" Patrick Wensink** — A comic masterpiece about the fast food industry, booze, and the necessity to choose happiness over work and security. **372 pages $15**

BB-142 **"Please Do Not Shoot Me in the Face" Bradley Sands** — A novel in three parts, *Please Do Not Shoot Me in the Face: A Novel*, is the story of one boy detective, the worst ninja in the world, and the great American fast food wars. It is a novel of loss, destruction, and--incredibly--genuine hope. **224 pages $12**

BB-143 **"Santa Steps Out" Robert Devereaux** — Sex, Death, and Santa Claus ... The ultimate erotic Christmas story is back. **294 pages $13**

BB-144 **"Santa Conquers the Homophobes" Robert Devereaux** — "I wish I could hope to ever attain one-thousandth the perversity of Robert Devereaux's toenail clippings." - Poppy Z. Brite **316 pages $13**

BB-145 **"We Live Inside You" Jeremy Robert Johnson** — "Jeremy Robert Johnson is dancing to a way different drummer. He loves language, he loves the edge, and he loves us people. These stories have range and style and wit. This is entertainment... and literature."- Jack Ketchum **188 pages $11**

BB-146 **"Clockwork Girl" Athena Villaverde** — Urban fairy tales for the weird girl in all of us. Like a combination of Francesca Lia Block, Charles de Lint, Kathe Koja, Tim Burton, and Hayao Miyazaki, her stories are cute, kinky, edgy, magical, provocative, and strange, full of poetic imagery and vicious sexuality. **160 pages $10**

BB-147 **"Armadillo Fists" Carlton Mellick III** — A weird-as-hell gangster story set in a world where people drive giant mechanical dinosaurs instead of cars. **168 pages $11**

BB-148 **"Gargoyle Girls of Spider Island" Cameron Pierce** — Four college seniors venture out into open waters for the tropical party weekend of a lifetime. Instead of a teenage sex fantasy, they find themselves in a nightmare of pirates, sharks, and sex-crazed monsters. **100 pages $8**

BB-149 **"The Handsome Squirm" by Carlton Mellick III** — Like Franz Kafka's *The Trial* meets an erotic body horror version of *The Blob*. **158 pages $11**

BB-150 **"Tentacle Death Trip" Jordan Krall** — It's *Death Race 2000* meets H. P. Lovecraft in bizarro author Jordan Krall's best and most suspenseful work to date. **224 pages $12**

BB-151 **"The Obese" Nick Antosca** — Like Alfred Hitchcock's *The Birds*... but with obese people. **108 pages $10**

BB-152 **"All-Monster Action!" Cody Goodfellow** — The world gave him a blank check and a demand: Create giant monsters to fight our wars. But Dr. Otaku was not satisfied with mere chaos and mass destruction.... **216 pages $12**

BB-153 **"Ugly Heaven" Carlton Mellick III** — Heaven is no longer a paradise. It was once a blissful utopia full of wonders far beyond human comprehension. But the afterlife is now in ruins. It has become an ugly, lonely wasteland populated by strange monstrous beasts, masturbating angels, and sad man-like beings wallowing in the remains of the once-great Kingdom of God. **106 pages $8**

BB-154 **"Space Walrus" Kevin L. Donihe** — Walter is supposed to go where no walrus has ever gone before, but all this astronaut walrus really wants is to take it easy on the intense training, escape the chimpanzee bullies, and win the love of his human trainer Dr. Stephanie. **160 pages $11**